DISORIENTALISM

KYOKO YOSHIDA
DISORIENTALISM

Dear Fran,
It's so nice to see you again in London!
Good luck at Keio.

27/2/2016

VAGABOND PRESS | PROSE

Acknowledgments: Earlier versions of some stories first appeared in the following publications: "Clarity" in *Outerbridge*, #27, 1998; "The Eastern Studies Institute" in *The Crab Orchard Review*, Spring/Summer, 1998; "The Movie Dog" in *The Western Humanities Review*, Summer, 1998; "A Bus Trip" in *The Distillery*, July, 2000; "Kyoto Panorama Project" in *The Massachusetts Review*, XLI, No. 4, 2000-01; "Chick Sexing School, or How Our Dead Grandfather Summoned Us to Japan" in *Red Cedar Review*, Winter, 2000-01; "Number 2 Pencils for the White Cat" in *The Bibliophilos*, Spring, 2001; "Between the Imperial Garden and Temple Street" in *Cimarron Review*, #139, Spring, 2002; "The Source of My Blue" in *Chelsea*, #72, December, 2002; "Marsupial, the Lowly Mammal" in *Panic Americana*, #8, 2003; "Borrowing Books" in *Panic Americana*, #8, 2003; "Mr. Volker" in *The Cream City Review*, #28.2, 2004; "Milk Bath" in *Nethra*, Vol. 3-8, 2005; "A Goldfish Galaxy" in *Beloit Fiction Journal*, #21, Spring, 2008.

First published 2014 by Vagabond Press
PO Box 958 Newtown NSW 2042 Australia
www.vagabondpress.net

©Kyoko Yoshida, 2013

Cover image: ©Takanori Ishizuka ©Dokuro Kogyo
Untitled, 2013, 240 x 280 x 300 cm, urethane, latex, TV monitor and others at Dokuyo Stationery shop, Tokyo.
Courtesy of nca | nichido contemporary art

Designed and typeset by Michael Brennan
in Adobe Garamond 12/17

All rights reserved. No part of this publication may be reproduced, stored in a retrieval system or transmitted in any form or by any means electronic, mechanical, photocopying or otherwise without the prior permission of the publisher. The information and views set out in this book are those of the author(s) and do not necessarily reflect the opinion of the publisher.

ISBN 978-1-922181-17-6

Contents

The Movie Dog 9
Squirrel Heaven 13
The Eastern Studies Institute 19
Mr. Volker 28
Borrowing Books 33
Kyoto Panorama Project 37
Marsupial, the Lonely Mammal 58
A Bus Trip 61
Octavia 66
A Goldfish Galaxy 78
Chick Sexing School 83
Number 2 Pencils for the White Cat 112
The Source of My Blue 116
Milk Bath 122
Between the Imperial Garden and Temple Street 143
Dreamcave 150
They Did Not Read the Same Books 154
Clarity 159
My Earshell Gondolier 187

For Milwaukee

In memory of Sheila Roberts (1937-2009)

the movie dog

When Sokobon was five, he wanted a dog. Mamabon took him to a movie in which a herd of puppies were running around from beginning to end. He wanted that puppy in the movie, a black-spotted coach dog that ran after your carriage for miles and miles. A little pup you could take along everywhere.

Somebody told him that if you wanted a dog, you should not tell your parents because it would never work; you ought to keep telling them that you want a little brother until you get a dog.

But Sokobon knew the little brother thing did not work, either. His friend Paragon had tried that spell on her parents already. When she learned that they had arranged to adopt a Korean baby for lonely Paragon, it was too late to confess to them that what Paragon had really wanted was a fluffy mew-mew tumbleweed kitten to play with, not the ugly hairless roaring creature to compete with for parental attention.

So Sokobon thought it would be best just to be honest and say that he wanted a movie dog.

"A movie dog?" Papabon raised his eyes from the evening paper.

Sokobon nodded standing patiently in front of him. "I'll be good. I'll take care of the dog."

Papabon stared at Sokobon for a while and then returned to his newspaper, saying, "You can have a video. Then you'll be able to watch it a million times."

"No!" Sokobon raised his voice. "I'm not talking about the dog movie. I'm talking about the movie dog. I want a puppy."

Mamabon detected the noise and came out of the kitchen, wiping her hands on her apron. "Why not, Papabon? If he'll be a good boy, we can get the movie dog for Christmas."

Papabon unwillingly nodded. He looked bitter whenever he capitulated to Mamabon, for he loved her too much.

Sokobon circled around Mamabon jumping and waving. "Movie dog. Movie dog."

Christmas came. Sokobon had been a very good boy: he had minded his evil babysitter; he had put his toys away by himself; he had never forgotten to wash his hands with soap whenever he came in from outside; he had gone to bed at eight sharp. Sokobon knew that Papabon and Mamabon had put his movie dog under their Christmas tree. There was a huge box nicely wrapped with a bow, quivering and quaking occasionally. When Sokobon unwrapped the gift, his dream puppy would bounce out of the box, jump onto his lap and lick his sugarcoated face, wagging its tail like a propeller. It would be a boy dog. He would name it Bonbon.

Something rustled inside the box. His parents nodded at him and Sokobon rushed to the tree. When he opened the box, a dark furry thing sluggishly walked out like a somnambulic nutria. It was two feet long, almost a foot wide, and had a fat boxy trunk. Its round face lacked expression, and it was cross-eyed. It had a very short neck and legs like a wild boar, but it was covered with thick, blackish curly hair.

It sniffed twice looking at Sokobon. It was a dog, anyway.

Without a word, the three watched it shambling to the TV set in the living room.

"This is not the movie dog," Sokobon mumbled and sat on the carpet cradling his knees in his arms. His eyes were cast down at his toes and grew larger and larger. He had to raise his face before water dropped out of them because he did not want to break his parents' hearts as they had his.

Mamabon looked at Papabon.

"Why, Sokobon," said Papabon jumping out of the couch and speaking briskly like a lying salesman, "This *is* the movie dog!"

Sokobon's eyebrows gathered even closer.

"Look, Sokobon!" Papabon trotted to the dark creature that was staring at the blank TV screen. He grabbed the short stiff tail of the dog and twisted it counterclockwise.

Then its sleepy eyes turned vivid. Its jaws seemed almost smiling. As Papabon rotated the tail, its eyes glowed brighter like a bicycle headlamp with a dynamo on a wheel. Light radiated from its fully opened eyes, whose beams projected two round illuminations around the TV set. The creature sat so that the floodlights stayed on the white wall above the TV. As its eyes turned square, the two spotlights on the wall transformed into one big rectangle. There was a flat image of a lion roaring behind a circled ribbon on the wall.

"See?" Papabon looked at his son showing his teeth. "Fun, isn't it?" But Sokobon looked even sadder.

"Oh, I know what you want," Papabon said and began to twist the dog's tail clockwise. The image on the wall stopped and the dog opened its jaws. Its mouth was torn up to its ears like a nutcracker or a snake swallowing an egg. The jaws opened so wide that its nose was above its eyes. The upper jaw turned over above its forehead and the lower jaw dropped to its forelegs with its lolling tongue. As Papabon kept twisting the tail, the jaws reached its trunk exposing its fleshy esophagus inside out. Steam rose. Still grinning at Sokobon, Papabon thrust his free hand into its stomach and exchanged video tapes. Then he rotated the tail counterclockwise again.

Soon the shades of those black-spotted coach dogs were dashing across the living room wall along with merry orchestra music.

But nobody paid attention to it anymore because Sokobon was crying like a fire alarm.

squirrel heaven

I'VE DECIDED THE REASON WHY I'VE NEVER SEEN A DEAD squirrel is that squirrels have a secret garden where they die, which, like a black hole, would instantaneously swoosh them into the squirrel heaven, where nuts and pizza crusts are abundant. But one day I finally come across a dead squirrel curled up in the grass at the foot of an oak tree near the Field Museum. The grass is a round patch, as though it has grown just to accommodate this squirrel's death. The squirrel has a dead face—a half-open eye, a dusty nuzzle and deteriorating gums—but the fur is still clean and the body undamaged. I take out my handkerchief, look around to see if anyone is watching, spread it next to the squirrel, brush the dirt off its face with a wisp of soft grass, scoop the body and wrap it up in the cloth, knotting its diagonal edges. I do not put the wrap in my bag. I clutch the knots and carry it home like a purse heavy with silver coins.

The rule is not not to eat animal meat. The rule is not to kill. So when we encounter a dead doe on the road, we express our gratitude to Earth and eat it. We must eat it so that life is not wasted. When we stumble upon a dead pigeon in the park, we thank Heaven and pluck it. Thus I've eaten rabbits, weasels, and raccoons. Many birds whose names I don't know. But I've never eaten a squirrel because I haven't set eyes on a dead squirrel before. There are so many squirrels around, all of them alive—fat and fast and alive everywhere. I must confess that when we go without meat for weeks, I start dreaming about the sweet tenderness of squirrel flesh. So many times my mouth has watered at the sight of those November fat squirrel buttocks. But squirrels never came to us dead until I found one near the Field Museum.

When I tell my mother I've found a dead squirrel, she immediately gets herself busy. She sends my brother off for acorns. My father cuts its tail off as a keepsake and starts skinning and gutting the creature. I light some incense and bring the bell. When my brother comes back with a handful of acorns, we sit at the table together and crush their shells. The acorns are wrapped tightly in a piece of tea towel, and I hold on to the wrytail of the towel, securing the wrap on a phonebook for my brother to thump the nuts with the kitchen mallet. We both remain quiet concentrating so as not to smash my fingers. Then the acorns are smeared with the fresh spices my mother has just ground in the mortar and stuffed into the squirrel's now hairless belly. While we wait sitting at the table in front of the oven, we tell our squirrel stories to each other occasionally ringing the bell, and it turns out it is the first time for any of us to have dead squirrel, except for my mother, who, as a child, grabbed a dead squirrel when she stuck her hand into a tree hole. It was early spring, my mother recalls, and the squirrel was still lukewarm, but its heart had stopped beating. It was a tiny, skinny squirrel. She remembers her mother put so many acorns in its hungry belly it almost burst in the oven.

I did once see a squirrel come close to death. This squirrel wanted to cross Belmont Street, darting underneath an SUV, and was nearly run over. The rear tire caught the tail fur and the creature tumbled round and round in front of the running tire. I was the only pedestrian next to the car. I was ready to scream, my hands pressing against my face. *No, not in front of my eyes, I wouldn't be able to swallow the consequences.* The squirrel rolled three times and finally dashed back to my side of the street, looking cute and stupid like any squirrel, like nothing had happened, and climbed up an oak tree. That is the squirrel story I contribute.

We each take a limb or the neck and share the trunk together. I am surprised it tastes exactly the way I imagined it would taste, but I did not imagine the small bones would be crunchy and edible. The acorns are the hardest to finish, bitter, hard, and dry. We masticate without a word.

Outside the window, my eyes search for live squirrels. I dream of fluffy tails fast funambulating on the telephone wires in the backyard, but I see none. *What if,* an apprehension grows as I chew on, *what if this is the beginning of the end?* The beginning of an epidemic, for instance? What if we see no more live squirrels dashing around, sticking out their tails from dumpsters? What if all the squirrels we are going to come across from now on will be dead squirrels because I discovered the secret garden where they gather to die?

A simple consequence: we will never worry about our food; we will eat nothing but squirrels for the rest of our lives. We will be overloaded with protein so our piss will smell strange. My brother and I will have to gather acorns every day. Someday my fingers will get smashed. And what if we cannot finish all the dead squirrels we find? It's been a while since we gave up our summer road trips. We just couldn't finish a dozen roadkills every day. Now we take planes and trains. The Scriptures do not tell us what to do with surplus dead animals. Heaven has never rained dead squirrels upon us.

I will bury the squirrel's skull under the round patch of grass tomorrow.

In the past, the rule applied to people, too. The rule was universal. The Scriptures value every form of life. When you set eyes on a dead grandmother, you did not waste her life. But as we moved to cities, it became difficult not to waste our dead, and the elders decided to make an exception. Consequently, I've seen a dead grandmother but never eaten one.

Now if we keep finding too many dead squirrels, we may have to give up eating squirrels altogether, making it an exception. Then the municipal hygiene office will organize regular cleanups of the squirrel corpses that perpetually materialize. Squirrel collection trucks will thread streets and alleys, chiming the squirrel collection music. Each truck will be equipped with a dustpan and a motorized broom. At stops, its rear lid will open up, producing the steel dustpan as wide as the truck itself on the ground, and the broom, or more of a huge deck brush resembling a baleen mustache, will come down to rake up the squirrel corpses, now a bunch of dusty furballs tossed up with cigarette stubs and candywrappers and crumpled pages of tabloid newspapers. When the lid flips open again and the dustpan heavy with the carcass meat lifts, pedestrians will get a glimpse of the rodential purgatory flame, where the waste is tossed. In a flash, the lid will shut tightly before we actually see the fur catching fire, and off the truck will go to the next collection spot, resuming the merry music, the dirge to send the innocent off to Heaven, and spewing crisp fumes into the air from its smokestack. The odor will tempt the heathens to grill meat for dinner, causing more lives to be wasted at the meat factories. We will have to witness squirrel lives and all sorts of other lives getting wasted. My heart throbs at the idea. It just doesn't sound right. We might have to move to a high-rise apartment downtown so as not to set eyes on the carcasses covering Earth, but then that means the end of accidental meat consumption. We will all live meatless until a clueless bird jumbles itself in the ventilation system, which may or may not happen once in several years. The elders will prohibit us to play on the ground, so I will have to hang around with kids from the high-rise who are not the most sympathetic kind of people to begin with. We will have to take a special masked vehicle to go to school. We will have to scurry down our way whenever on the ground, averting our eyes from the Truth, meaning that we too become hypocrites like the heathens. Some people who've been making fun of us will ridicule us even more as we run down the street, and we will have to leave the city all together someday.

the eastern studies institute

In the courtyard of the Eastern Studies Institute, geometrically arranged are a Spanish-style fountain with a stone stem, three lines of flower beds framed with Turkish blue tiles, and a Dr. Harada. Today he is a panda bear. Last month, he was a Rasputin. It is not Harada Ken'ichiro himself, of course, the famous historian from the beginning of the twentieth century, the founder of the institute; it is a bronze bust of Harada Ken'ichiro mounted five foot high on a granite pedestal. He has been poured on by rain, scorched by the shimmering sun, and bitten by savage frost. Every student who passes in front of Dr. Harada bows to him out of respect. They cannot help embellishing Dr. Harada every month. Every other month, he is removed from the pedestal for regular bathing while a student stands in his place with his face painted bronze green.

People recall time and events with Dr. Harada's costumes. Dr. Togo, Assistant Professor, knocked his Celica's bumper against a pole in December 1991, when Dr. Harada was posing as a Lenin at the collapse of the Soviet Union. A white shirt congealed with plaster equipped him with arms for the first time in his postmortem bust life. It was surely February in 1989 when Ms. Sakamoto, the ever-stressed secretary, stayed in the hospital for a gastric ulcer because people well remember Dr. Harada was a Hirohito in commemoration of the Emperor's funeral. Dr. Harada was a moai, whose cardboard head extension majestically soared, commanding the pink tulip buds in the courtyard, when some ignorant members of the board planned to display Dr. Harada in a glass case at the university museum. Students erected a barricade across the gate and the attempt ended in failure.

The main building of the Eastern Studies Institute has white mortar walls, orange tiled roofs, black lattice windows, and a small viewing tower. The four-storied Andalusian architecture stands out, surrounded by a thicket in the traditional Japanese residential neighborhood at the foot of Mt. Yoshida. In summer, the cool shade lures the pedestrians into the entrance lobby of the institute, which, however, is already full of the local dogs lying flat on the gray marble floor dangling their tongues.

The Eastern Studies Institute was founded in the early twentieth century with part of the compensation money for the Sino-Japanese War in 1895. The Shimonoseki Treaty brought two hundred million silver taels to Japan. By virtue of the Eastern Studies Institute, Japan could compete with China in Sinology. The institute owns a rare collection of books and documents, many of which were purchased from China with the compensation money. A double exploitation. The collection is stored in the stacks, located in the heart of the institute, into which only the staff librarians and the tenured faculty are allowed. The storage is four stories high, in the form of a giant spiral staircase, with a vast, square wellhole in the center. A gentle slope encloses the wellhole in squares with fifteen right angles. Ascending the slope counterclockwise, you find a railing on your left, an aged, shiny mahogany rail, and there are bookshelves and the wall on your right. At your feet, the tilting floor is inlaid with thick blocks of glass. Those afraid of heights tiptoe over the transparent squares on the top floor.

Since all the floors are leaning, the bookshelves, as you may well imagine, are tilted, too. Each shelf is twenty meters long, the length of each wall. Books are naturally packed tightly together as gravity neatly squeezes the books to the right end of the shelves. To return a book to a shelf, you put it at the left end of the shelf. The more often a book is called, the further to the left it is located on the shelf. The books at the right end of the shelves, in most cases, have never been in circulation since the institution was established. But when you need them—and this is the problem about these bookshelves—you must pull out the book with all your might, and even that is not enough sometimes: there are quite a few spineless books at the right end of the sloped shelves. Another problem is that you have to go all the way up to the end of the shelf to return books. Hammy calves are an occupational hazard of the institution's librarians. This is another fight against gravity, especially when they have to push a cart on the slippery glass slopes to reshelf too many books. Once, when Dr. Harada was a Bruce Lee—that is, in August of 1973—Miss Akiyama lost her grip and the cart slipped back and smashed against the corner of the slope, sprinkling the books. The empty cart roared on to the starting point, where she had to start all over again, but could not, because her left ankle, run over by the cart, was broken.

Another major danger, the temptation to jump off the fourth floor into the wellhole, is so irresistible that the library produces a few deaths every year. In the center of the ground floor, there is a heavy ebony working table surrounded by heaps of books. The table is the only empty space on the floor. It is a shiny black hole that draws in those who look down over the railing.

It was a muggy evening in August 2005 when the Eastern Studies Institute produced an unexpected death. The annual suicides of librarians and faculty members are expected. Their deaths are always welcome because they lower the average age of the staff and provide new positions for those who have been waiting. Applicants are always waiting in line in front of the Eastern Studies Institute. Snack and drink vendors sell expensive rice balls and tepid tea along the line. At night, several campfires form an exotic zodiac in front of the institute's gate. Whenever a cedar coffin exits the Spanish façade followed by a dozen mourning people, the swarm of waiting applicants, those the staff refer to as *the waiters*, throng around the coffin like puppets without knee joints (for they are crippled due to standing in line for an indeterminable length of time) cheering, clapping, tripping and shoving each other to check which position has become vacant. Then those who are qualified gather silently around the front door.

But that day, when a plywood coffin came out of the building, crossing the courtyard, passing by the small Spanish fountain, and the rose beds, and then Dr. Harada, the eyes outside the façade sparkled only for a moment before they found out the corpse was not their savior. It was a Chinese graduate student found dead by the librarians with his head cracked open like a ripe pomegranate on the solid ebony table.

His name was Mu Wai and he was from Xian, formerly known as Changan, the metropolis of the first millennium. His academic concern was to reproduce colloquial Tibetan of the early eleventh century through its phonetic transcription in the Chinese ideograms recorded in parts of the Dunhuang Documents. Studying Sinology in foreign lands was his destiny; the Dunhuang Documents, torn into parts and grabbed by the colonial powers, now exist only outside China.

Mu Wai had been in exile from Paris to St. Petersburg, from London to Hong Kong, from Tokyo to Kyoto in research of the lost Tibetan sounds. His Chinese translation of Dr. Harada's major works provided him with the funding. He had never forgotten to bow to him in the courtyard. Of course, he was a member of Dr. Harada's apparel committee.

When Mu Wai was found dead, flat on the working table with his head cracked open, he was holding a book in his right hand, *Xiyouji*—a novel from the Ming Period, one of the *Four Fantastics* of Chinese Literature. Based on High Priest Xuanzang's pilgrimage from Changan to Magadha from 627 to 645 in pursuit of *Mahaprajnaparamitasutra,* the *Great Sutra of the Perfection of Transcendent Wisdom.* The novel tells the fantastic adventures of the three guardian creatures protecting him from the eighty-one evil monsters in his passage to India. The water spirit, the pig monster and the golden witty monkey, our favorite mimic picaroon, the monkey king. The book is illustrated: the monkey jumps around High Priest Xuanzang. Somersault. Somersault. Such a magical, mighty monkey he is. Mu Wai heard, watched and read the tale hundreds of times in dozens of versions.

The copy in Mu Wai's dead hand was one of the two copies of the oldest edition in existence. The other was somewhere in Paris. Mu Wai had known the Eastern Studies Institute owned one. But he had not known it actually existed until he found its card by mere chance, searching through the card catalog looking for other books. Ever since, he had been haunted by it. The stack room had metamorphosed into a gourd, which *Xiyouji* got imprisoned in, the gourd that sucks the golden monkey. All Mu Wai had fancied at first was to have a glance at the spines of the volumes. Just to make sure they really existed. When he had snuck into the top floor of the stack room, however, after hiding and holding his breath behind the booth by the door—the only hole into the gourd—a sudden realization of his true intention came to Mu Wai. Sucking in the silent whispers, weeping, and wooing of the prints, he reeled back, seized by a bibliomanic dizziness. He grasped the railings with both hands and balanced himself on the partially transparent, tilted floor. The wellhole was windowless except for one big skylight, practically the whole ceiling, which filtered the slanted remains of the setting summer sun casting zigzag lights on the eastern shelves. The bottom floor was dark. He staggered to the fiction section and soon found the shelf the card had indicated. It was the top shelf. The book was at the far right end of the shelf. No one had called for *Xiyouji* for years. Mu Wai dragged a ladder, propped it up against the shelves, climbed up, brushed the spines with his index finger, and set his hand on the spine of the first volume.

Then he tugged at it with all his might.

The next day after the police left, another of the malevolent summer nights came. The dense heat stagnated in the wellhole, gradually steaming the corpse that still lay on its back on the ebony table. Its arms were bent stiff in rigor mortis with its book-gripping hand in front of its motionless chest. Meibiao alone kept vigil over the corpse. He is from Nanjing and was the dead's best friend amongst many Chinese in the institute. Meibiao is a beautiful, lofty young man, just like his name, Lovely Tiger Fur, suggests. He sat in a folding chair by the table, staring at the air between the corpse's open eyes and the title cover of *Xiyouji*. The broken head was covered with cotton gauze. Flies buzzed into the wellhole, and every time a fly alighted on the corpse's nostril or eyeball, Meibiao stood up to wave it away with the evening newspaper he had grabbed on his way in the lobby of the international students' dormitory.

The next morning undertakers carried in a coffin, and a couple of librarians and Meibiao helped them to remove the corpse. Before the undertakers closed the coffin, a librarian with a flowery apron hesitantly mentioned the book in the corpse's right hand. The undertakers gave her a vacant look, for they had taken it as a souvenir for the dead on its long journey to the netherworld. The other librarian shook her head and explained what the book was and how much they had tried to undo the grip in vain. They looked at the corpse's hand. Its well-trimmed nails had lodged into the fibers of the covers. The undertakers tugged at the book in turn. Then they made Meibiao try. The book stuck fast to the hand like it was a part of the corpse. One undertaker whipped out a pair of pliers from his jumpsuit pocket. The fingers snapped like dry twigs. He handed the book to the perplexed librarian and started to nail the lid on the coffin.

The undertakers told the librarians and Meibiao that the severe climate allowed the corpse to be kept no longer, so it would be cremated and its ashes would be returned to China in an urn. The three nodded. Meibiao then realized he did not know where in Xian Mu Wai came from.

On their way to the undertakers' van parked at the gate, they crossed the courtyard. It was half-past noon. The yard was full of white light. The sun pressed them hard against the concrete earth. Meibiao and the undertakers stooped as they carried the coffin. Passing Dr. Harada, Meibiao asked the others to stop for a moment. That day, Dr. Harada wore a pair of round sunglasses, a flat Panama hat, and a lei of pink synthetic hibiscus. On the pedestal it said "UKULELE." Meibiao bobbed his head at the tropical Dr. Harada. Then they headed for the gate crowded with waiters.

mr. volker

It was when we visited a city in North America whose name sounded similar to *milk*. Or more like *Milkyway*. Instead people drank beer there. No, people drank milk, but they preferred squeaky dairy products to the liquid, and beer best of all. Two men ice-fishing almost drowned themselves in the lake the day before, the icebreak day approaching.

Everyone we met asked us why did you come here? Why Milkyway? There's nothing here during the winter. We always replied: well, we didn't mean to. Then people would look hurt a little. People had fairly solid work ethics, but sometimes their minds seemed to drift off, especially during the winter when the gray lake and the leaden sky seem to blend into one, while the factories in the south poured more fume to mingle the two. On such days, people seemed to stay in bed all day and enjoy their gray nightmares, or go out and shoot some other people, or go out to a hardware store, buy a hatchet and chop up some more people, or go out to a hardware store, buy a shovel and shovel some snow instead.

So what are you? a man at a bar stared at us and asked, since we neither stay in bed, shoot people, chop people up, nor shovel snow.

We translate letters, we told him. We translate letters from one language to another, or sometimes from one language to several others. We cannot do any lengthier translations than letters, because we have to work standing at podiums. You see, we pointed at our hip, it's difficult to sit and write for us. Then we were telling him of the letter we translated the week before we came to Milkyway—a North Korean cabaret owner in Osaka reported a case of three Filipino dancers missing. Letter writing requires subtle techniques of concealment and revelation, letter translating even more so. We had paid most attention to making sure that the letter reader would never figure out whether the three Filipino dancers were legal workers or not, and whether these employees (legal or illegal) disappeared voluntarily or were kidnapped. What we did was we would each start a sentence for the other to finish. That's how we worked.

Then the man said, okay, it's my turn to tell you two young ladies a story. I was shoveling the snow instead yesterday and my twin sister came home from the hardware store with a new hatchet and a shovel. You know, our hardware store is located at a solitary corner. Sometimes people get to use their new hatchet even before they reach their home or their friends' home, but anyway, my sister told me that she saw a huge hare with antlers on her way home. It wore a summer coat, grayish brown, at least twice as large as an adult hare, and it was extremely muscular like a bobcat. It dashed out of the shrub in front of the hardware store, shook off some snow, and their eyes met for a second, my twin sister and the hare—its eyes had this wild look, she told me, or the look of the once conscientious being gone wild. Big eyes and strong jaws. It wore a pair of fully developed antlers though one of them was missing a third of it. They stared at each other for a second and the hare went back into the shrub.

That's Mr. Volker the great jackalope king of hares, we said.

Yes, exactly, that's what I told my twin sister: Sis', that's Mr. Volker the great jackalope king of hares.

Why didn't she use her new hatchet? we asked.

See? That's what I asked her, too! Why didn't you use your hatchet? That's what it is for!

But again, we don't know, we said to the man, because you started the story and your twin sister finished it. How do we know whether your sister really encountered Mr. Volker the great jackalope king of hares?

But, well, you have to believe us! I stopped shoveling, went down to the basement, picked up my old hatchet, and my sister and I went back to the hardware store at the solitary corner, we each had a hatchet and a shovel. The hardware store is sort of located on the hill, commanding the lake, under the freeway, so it's dark during the day. That day, even darker, since it had snowed.

Which shrub did it come out of, I mean Mr. Volker the great jackalope king of hares? I asked my twin sister.

There. She pointed to the tallest one by the shop door.

Then the doors swung open and a tall woman with broad shoulders and short blond hair walked into the bar. She had a soiled shovel in her thick hand.

You talking about Mr. Volker the great jackalope king of hares? she said to the man.

Yes, sister, I'm telling these young ladies the story of Mr. Volker the great jackalope king of hares.

So what are you? the twin sister stared at our hip and asked.

We are letter translators, we said, adjusting our standing posture against the bar, stepping forward and backward like a dancing couple while skillfully avoiding entangling our four legs.

But anyway, the man resumed the story: we poked the bush in front of the hardware store, and

And the hare came out, the twin sister took over his sentence: so we held it down with our shovels on the back of its neck. The hare was so strong that it was a two-man job just to hold it down. Then we struck its antlers with our hatchets, one for each. The hare's eyes became bloodshot; its white bobtail quivered. After so many strokes, the antlers dropped off—they just shed off like dead leaves. The hare still had that wild look—did you tell these ladies about its peculiar wild look, brother?—but it was mixed with something new, a sort of relief, a mixture of grief, agony, and relief.

We lifted our shovels. And the hare dashed off, this time out to the parking lot under the highway. Its coat soon vanished into the gray slush of the parking lot. The antlers remained. So there's no Mr. Volker the great jackalope king of hares any more in Milkyway. Not any more. Except in souvenir cards from Milkyway. Thus, the sister finished the story.

We were standing at the bar because we couldn't sit, you see, because of our hip. We stared at the sister, her pale eyes, her strong jaws, and her shovel soiled with gray snow. We thought of the sense of relief Mr. Volker the great jackalope king of hares had when it found it was no more the great jackalope king of hares. We looked at each other. From her coat pocket, the sister drew out an antler. It was shaped like an aged bonsai pine tree. It had apparently grown in torment over years. The top one-third was missing, the cut still edgy and uneven. It fit in our small hand, and at its root, a tuft of heather brown hair remained. We looked at the twins. They looked at us and said, one starting and the other finishing the sentence, why did you come here? Why Milkyway? We looked down at the small antler in our hand, touched its pointy branches with the tips of our fingers, and said, well, we didn't mean to.

borrowing books

ONE NIGHT KENNETH VISITED HIS LOVE, BARBARA, AND showed her a novel he had borrowed from Jenny, then jealous Barbara said to him that Kenneth was lucky to have so many female friends; she didn't have any male friends to borrow a book from. Kenneth pointed at himself and said how about himself, he was a good friend of hers, but she replied that "good friends" don't fuck, a remark which made Kenneth truly sad because he had believed Barbara was his best friend and he himself had always tried to be her best friend, too. This incident disappointed Kenneth greatly.

Next morning, when he woke up in Barbara's bed, a wonderful idea cracked in his mind: he should sleep equally with every female friend of his to prove "good friends" do fuck. He was convinced that Barbara would then realize she was the very best among his female friends if Kenneth slept with all of his female friends.

Kenneth started to work on his idea. First, he had to make a list of women to do. Ninety-eight names lined up on his list. They were all his good friends. He imagined the sight of ninety-eight women standing in a row in front of his bedroom door. He was almost giving up this dreary project before he compromised by picking those who had lent him books. This new rationale trimmed the number from ninety-eight to ten, yet Kenneth was not satisfied, for some women excluded from the list were obviously closer friends than the ten book-lenders. So Kenneth made another list of women who made better friends than the ten women whom he had borrowed books from. The total number of his female friends on the two lists turned out to be twenty-three, which seemed a reasonable number to execute his plan.

Soon Kenneth found out how easy it was to undress his good female friends. None of them had said no so far. Many of them undressed themselves voluntarily as if they had been waiting for this moment. A couple of women became upset after the thing was over, but as far as they had willingly done it, Kenneth did not care.

He assumed it would not take long before he crossed off all the names on his list.

To finish off his plan quickly, Kenneth could have done two or three women at once, but he never did because what he was doing was not about promiscuity but about friendship.

Of those who had not lent him a book, Kenneth would ask, "May I borrow your book?"

Everyone replied happily, "Sure! Which book?" Kenneth bonked them instead of answering that question.

By the time he copulated with thirteen out of the twenty-three women, an odd thing began to happen: they wouldn't lend him books any more. They would buy Zippo lighters for him instead of lending him books. They threatened his peace of mind with vacuum cleaners and bags of groceries. They demanded that he take them to the movies, to the beach at sunset, to French restaurants, anywhere they had never been with Kenneth. They had arguments when they run into each other in his room. A few women began to use the word *commitment*, which baffled Kenneth. Many of them requested him to squeeze their breasts and flip their skirts again.

He said that he had no time to waste.

Then they would complain, saying, "Don't you love me any more? What was that last Tuesday night when you made love to me so passionately?"

He would say, "No! I didn't make love to you! I just wanted to make sure I could borrow a book from you," and go away.

Kenneth was getting exhausted. He badly needed to see Barbara, whom he had not seen for more than a month. He wanted to touch her velvety belly and to read together on her sofa, but he had to finish up with his "good female friends" first to prove his thesis. Kenneth was not a vigorous man. All the physical activities had emaciated him. When he finally fulfilled his mission, Kenneth was just skin and bone. He tottered to Barbara's apartment. She wasn't home. He waited for her in front of the door like an old dog. The passers-by cast suspicious glances at this man, who was trembling in the dewy night, squatting on the ground.

At last Barbara came home, holding a couple of books under her arm and a grocery bag in her hand. The books had classification labels on their spines. She must have stopped by the public library on her way home from work.

"What are you doing here?" Barbara asked, looking down at him while groping for the key in her coat pocket.

"May I borrow your book?" Kenneth said, still crouching.

"Sure! Which book?" she said, nonchalantly.

"*The Astronomic Almanac*," said Kenneth, failing to raise himself. Barbara jerked him up with her empty hand. She let him in, and right after she handed him *The Astronomic Almanac*, her fist knocked him down on the kitchen floor. She had known what he had been doing, of course.

Kenneth lost all his "good female friends" but succeeded in demonstrating that Barbara was his love and best friend: she loved him and lent him a book, too. Although she would not let him touch her for the following six months, they lived happily ever after.

kyoto panorama project

Y IS A STREET MUSICIAN, ARRESTED FOR AIDING AND *abetting a defector. I, X, am a stenographer on duty to record his every word behind bars. I am staying in the cell across from his. Y speaks every night. Although there is no way of his sensing the solar revolution, he starts his words everyday at nightfall.*

His voice is calm.

I.

Kyoto is a damned city, don't you think? Our capital of the millennium, the flower of Japonism, the highlight of tourism. Ah, she's an old hag.

Never stay too long in Kyoto, or that'll be our ruination. We're so young, yet already dotards, you and I. The city gnaws our youth. That is the curse of Kyoto.

You never notice how much you've aged, you are a busy man bustling about from Arashiyama to Higashiyama, but I can see the years flying by as I waste my days lingering around a telephone pole at Kojinguchi.

I wasn't like this before, believe me. My limbs were swift and nimble, I had a strong will, I'd beat asses I loathe, and I'd never lost my mind after drinks. But once I'm in Kyoto, I'm on the skids. Drowsiness is my permanent condition, my mind muddy, my skull cloudy inside. I've become weary of everything. Yet, deep down, I am a hysteric, screaming and stamping, my hair bristling up, my head sizzling, like trying to remain cool-faced when your bladder is about to explode.

It's all because of this place.

I'll whisper into your eyes, this is a city of nightmare, Kyoto is.

Many friends went psycho in Kyoto. Especially those who call themselves rock stars. They do go-go and they go gaga. That guitarist, E. Flat, smelled madness in the air out of the train at Kyoto Station. He refused to play but the agent forced him anyway, and on stage he gradually fell into a trance and never stopped playing, even after everything was over and other members of the band ripped away his Gibson and his fingers kept twisting and twitching in the air. He hanged himself in the stinking toilet of Kyoto Station.

Just look around on the street. It's a nut farm. The woman at the intersection won't budge an inch. She stands by the traffic signal all day long. The man with bloodshot eyes in the cantina is perpetually ranting at some imaginary coconut head. The boy in the city bus will loosen his pants to reveal his peanuts.

What makes them crazy is the deposit of murky air at the bottom of the Basin. Surrounded by mountains, not a breeze has blown since some capricious emperror decided to move in 1200 years ago. It was a capital mistake. We're breathing the same moldy air the ghosts and the demons, the clueless infant emperors and the cruel merchants, the dogs and the peasants exhaled. We're crammed in the same old blood-sucking basin where they lived, died and rotted, lived, died and rotted, lived, died and rotted, lived, died and rotted, lived, died and rotted….

Today is another day the refugees from all over head for Kyoto.

The first on the list are the academics—those pedantic con men—then follow skinhead merchants (call them priests if you please), the parricides & the pedophiles, the gamblers & the college applicants, the artsy types & the literary hacks, the militant pacifists & the melancholic right-wingers, the horny gourmands & the impotent alcoholics, the shopaholic princesses & the yellow-fever gaijins… they are all kindred. The city is packed with these creatures.

But do you know the king of refugees, the refugee among refugees?

Yes. Geniuses.

They get rejuvenated dramatically in Kyoto while we wrinkle up. They surely grow wild like tropical trees fertilized by heaps of the rotten mediocre refugees and the ashes of exhausted natives.

Once in a while I console myself with the thought that I'm becoming food for the geniuses, not for the squirrels. Well, perhaps not much difference, but that kind of feeling does help a bit. What is all this juice they suck from us for? How come they die young while we survive and enjoy our feeble fungible life?

We are guaranteed to live long no matter. We shall all therefore make every effort to die suffering in pain at least, because only the painful death will redeem our pointless lives.

I am longing to writhe in agony on my deathbed. I want to die suffering. At the very moment I die, I will regret my wish. On my deathbed, I'll regret the killing pain I wished for. As the pain becomes remorse I'll die damning myself. This is my wish.

And they'll dump my body in the River.

This is my life—and the lives of those unable to clear the Walls and escape this city.

Kyoto is surrounded by the Walls. Kyoto has no sky. The thick tall Walls block it. Many have recklessly tried to penetrate through the Walls. They've dug tunnels, they've pretended to be dead in coffins, they've flown on the kites....

Many died. Only a handful ever bolted over the Walls though there's no way of knowing, on this side of the Walls, if they made it alive or dead, to say nothing of whether or not they found happiness on the other side.

Our job is to put away the bodies shot by the Police Gunmen in the Tower, the candle shaped Kyoto Tower by the Station.

Tonight is another night when the Tower looms up in the pale footlights. A faint sound leaks from the other side of the Walls. The foreign music with its strange beat infects us with a spine-burning excitement of liberation.

It was a night like this when he decided to bolt.

Yes, *him—loafer, liar, nincompoop*, whatever names we call him by. For now, let us just call him Z.

We were roaming around the Tower and Z bragged he could make it through the Walls. Like a magician. I laughed and said he'd better show us he really could.

Z chuckled and said, My plan is perfect. I shall fly the coop beautifully. You shall gnash your teeth.

Free or dead—no choice in between. This is the enchantment of taking chances.

He narrowed his slanted eyes and gazed over the walls.

And on a night of pouring rain, Z was running and rolling, chased by the searchlight of the Tower Police.

What happened to me? he cried. I'm the one supposed to fly the coop beautifully. How come I'm lying in the mud, hiding from the searchlight, sobbing and shuddering?

I shall no longer live. Time to die.

What ignominy.

Having run away from the Tower Police, Z trudged along by the Kamo River, on Kawabata Street looking for a place to die, and he stopped by the Sanjo-Ohashi Bridge.

Every bridge is an epitome of the world. We meet across the bridge, we embrace on the bridge, make love under the bridge and die beneath the bridge. The Sanjo-Ohashi Bridge has witnessed it all. On the right bank, couples are making out sitting at even intervals. Passers-by on the bridge are peeping at them, turning their eyes away from the lumpens who are making fire on the left bank. The bridge is crowded with pushcarts and bicycles, clochards and charlatans, vagabonds and dogs. Always dogs. And gulls gliding around for breadcrumbs. Looking down south from the bridge, the downtown is blurred in yellow dust, and up north the gentle slope of the Kitayama Mountains lie like a woman reclining on her side.

That night the bridge was deserted, except for dogs that followed him in pity. Many lamps were dead. The night airflow and the rain's reflection contoured the bridge's withered cypress railings. The blue searchlight of the Tower was penetrating the rain far in the south; the red lights of Kiyamachi were seducing men in the east. He stank of mud and he was trembling and crying. What a perfect bridge it was for a sloppy fugitive to jump off, to hang himself from, or to commit harakiri on. Any way you like.

Do it now before the rain washes your dirt away and makes you a new person.

He jumped. While falling in slow motion, the phantasmagoria of his bygone days passed by in his mind, edited in sepia, accompanied with gloomy Brahms fiddles and all.

My life wasn't too awful after all, was it? he thought, I think. Or was it not?

He didn't manage to die. He was bruised all over, but that was nothing.

He was sitting in the water of the Kamo River for a long while before he stood up in the ankle-deep water. The rain had gone before he knew it, a wind blew, clouds flowed and revealed a full moon.

A pale plump one.

Is it a revelation, some kind of illumination? he asked himself.

No, it's just a reflection. A satellite light.

What a fool he is. The Kamo River is a *maybe* river, a camoflowage. It's all about betraying our expectations. We won't be able to kill ourselves so long as we expect the Kamo River to kill us. At the Kamo River, we die only when we intend to live. I know anything about the Kamo River. My name is no pretense.

What's done cannot be undone. He has to make another escape plan. He has to give it another try.

Thus Y quits his confession for the rest of the night.

II.

There is no sky in Kyoto, but there are moons.

In winter, a new crescent slits the darkness at the zenith, dripping lucid blood and making a freezing cry.

In spring, cherry blossoms and a hazy moon contend with each other amid the ting-a-ling of the sake glasses and buzzing of the folks outside.

In summer, the smoke of fireworks on the River shades an eerie red half moon.

In fall, the full luminescent halo of a harvest moon floats over the Higashiyama Mountains.

At the sight of the moon, my daytime languor is momentarily mitigated. This worldly absurdness, the stifling daylight, my paralytic arms, the tedium of conversations—all becomes a lie under the gaze of our satellite.

And as I close my eyes, I feel myself as a body of discrete parts: I become blurred; I become you; I become *she*; I become *he*; and here is not Kyoto, here is there, the other side of the Walls, another country where we speak in another grammar.

I can't help strolling out every time I sniff the scent of that lunar vapor beaming from the ceiling.

I open my eyes upon the moon.

The night sea comes down to me—the sweet seawater seeps down into me, macerates me and diffuses me. The luscious liquor showers down upon me, luring me into lunatic euphoria.

Listen: the music from beyond the Walls is ebbing and flowing, flooding and spouting, rolling and swelling.... I listen, holding my breath, curling between the sheets.

Z is now toasting his humiliating failure, lilting a moon song at a booze stall on Kiyamachi Lane. Two glasses are enough to tint him pink. Licking the rice liquor that reflects the lunar luminescence, Z falls into a reverie—he is floating on the cold current. Drop by drop, sweet water lights up little candles in the bottom of his gut and melts his bones. He will let himself drift with the tide, weaving his way through waves of electric wires, a sea of telegraph trees, a jungle under the water—with his mouth slightly open, until his memory comes back—his fishhood memory.

Once upon a time, fish could fly.

He's convinced of that. He closes his eyes, and he finds himself at the bottom of the sea gazing up himself as an aquamarine mackerel quivering its opalescent fins, and flits through the trees up into the round moon. The exuberant drum beats shake the air beyond the Walls. His intoxicated brain is thumping at the beat.

I'm a fish.... I will be able to fly over the Walls....

The drum beats louder, his wings airy. The Walls approach.

Ah, I am flying over the Walls now....
Yes. Now.

Thus Y quits his confession for the rest of the night.

III.

His head throbs upon waking.

Z finds himself lying face down in the middle of the shopping arcade.

His clothes are stained and stink of rot. He's perhaps slept hugging a garbage bag. His spine crackles.

Will you get out of the way now that you're up?

Forcing his gummed-up eyes open, he grimaces at the source of the sharp voice. A tiny woman with a broom in her hand stands, glaring at him, ready to sweep the scum off.

He is dumbfounded, terror-struck.

Women in general appear beautiful at nightfall, but this one unashamedly so in broad daylight. He feels a mixture of a little admiration and a great deal of anxiety.

Ma...nay...

He makes desperate efforts to continue his words, but alas, he merely quivers out gasps.

What?

The tiny woman bangs the pavement with the handle of the broom.

What about your precious name? Like I care? You are lying in my way, stopping me from sweeping. I had to clean the front of the shop before Madame came, but this stinking drunkard, which is you, sir, in case you need any specification, was lying in my way and there was trash everywhere and, happy holidays! I was scolded by Madame, thank you very much, I won't be able to stay here because Madame isn't satisfied with my work anymore, so now what will you do to repay me for all the mess you've created?

It's a breathtaking spectacle, he thinks, she is beautiful and brutal. Insolence is a rare virtue.

No, I'm not talking of my name, I'm asking *your* name, he says.

Get out of my way and I'll tell you.

He scurries to the gutter on the other side of the street. The girl quietly clears the area he was occupying.

My name is Kyoto. K-Y-O-T-O. Use the same ideograms as Kyoto. I can't write them myself, though.

How pretty Kyoto is: her jet black hair is an absolute tousle, its length uneven—did she cut it by herself with her eyes closed?—her limbs are bony like drift twigs on the beach, her knees abraded. She is dressed in an obsolete black maid dress a bit too short for everything—especially the sleeves baring her wristbones. The dress's elbows are shiny, her lace apron yellowish, and her skin so fair that dirt shows.

Her eyes are dark azure, like the sky when Venus appears. Her lips, cheeks and nails are naturally bloody red. Surely a hot-blooded girl, he chuckles to himself.

What a surprise. Z quits drinking after that. He's been an idiot from the beginning, but this episode was just too good. We all laugh at him.

Z comes out of his den every day, crosses the Kamo River and heads for the shopping arcade with a guitar. He's a fish who plays the guitar.

A sightseeing bus passes by. People sigh that the sight of Kyoto from the height of the sightseeing bus is dazzling, almost blinding. A pretty furious looking little tour guide keeps a beady eye on the passengers so none of them will open the window. Once it's cracked open, the musty gas fills up the bus in an instant and the passengers will all turn airhead like popcorns.

Arriving at the arcade, Z kneels and kowtows three times, and twangs away at the guitar and sings.

It's a serenade at high noon. At the stale shopping arcade. Hee, hee, hee. Nobody's listening to him. Ah, what a joke, ha. Hey, what are you looking at, like you've got nothing to do with this? But you certainly are a part of this, aren't you? He's surely hopeless. Gee, you are hopeless. You have to laugh with me. Say, ha ha? I don't hear you. Say it again, ha ha? Louder!

All we can do is laugh. So laugh!

Indeed it's so droll some people drop some change for Z. He gets mad and throws the money back at them. He's too good for money.

For the first week, Z crosses the River, strums the guitar, sings his songs, circles around the shop like a tomcat in heat.

For the next week, he does pretty much the same.

For the third week, I think he does the same sort of thing.

On the last day of the seventh week of his pilgrimage, his prayers are answered and Kyoto gets kicked out of the shop at last.

Kyoto rushes out of the shop and she punches him right in the face. His face twitches with painful pleasure. He turns his left cheek to her, giggling. Kyoto ignores the offer and knees him in the guts. He falls still giggling. She now has nothing left but herself.

Back on his feet, Z takes her hand and walks her to the Riverbank. At night, the two sleep at the foot of the Bridge, holding each other.

Thus Y quits his confession for the rest of the night.

IV.

You know how to turn a sweater inside out.

If you turn your skin, flesh and fat inside out just like you do a sweater, you turn into a woman. You become a perfect woman, more real than any woman out there. Everybody knows it but no one dares to speak of it, this so-called open secret, and if you insist you've never heard of it, it's not that you've been ignorant but just oblivious.

Put a moldy comforter kept in the closet into water, and it will swoosh up into a white elephant—the same sort of esotericism.

Womanly women, sewing women, office women, anchor women—they are all fake. They are all men's women. Lucky enough if you could meet a genuine woman ever. Rarer is a genuine man.

The city is crowded with men's men—but this is another story, so I'll keep it for another time.

So coming back to Z. Only if his story had been told by XX, instead of XY, he could've been a genuine woman. I'm sorry about that, but we can't help it, can we?

But now he's got a woman at least. This time he thinks he's ready to bolt. It's easy as XYZ.

Z and Kyoto have been sticking flat to the Walls, pricking up their ears to listen to the beats from the other side. They never tire of the rhythm. The promenade by the Walls is famous for pervert lovers who love to embrace and caress each other while being watched by the Tower Police. Every five minutes when the Tower guard passes by, he looks daggers at the two. This is the twentieth time. The guard's eyes are bloodshot, full of suspicion. He withstands the temptation to trample them down like worms. He purrs and groans at them. Sweat streaks down on their backs. They stick to the Walls even flatter. It's such a silly sight, they look like a pair of pinned specimens. XY and YY.

When the guard passes them for the twenty-somethingth time, Z turns to Kyoto and says, Let's beat it.

Fabulous, replies Kyoto immediately, and right away the guard turns to glare at the two, but the guard's gorilla face only makes them burst out laughing. The guard trots away blushing.

Yes, Z's different from us. He's no genius, but he's wrapped in his sweater so slyly. He's an idiot, but now because of her, he can wear his orange sweater inside out, and pretend to be a tourist just off a bullet train. That's his plan.

Why do they remain untamed, I mean, the cats in Kyoto? I've seen and known cats in old capitals of the world, and I swear, cats have degenerated.

Where have they gone, those divine cats that scavenge in the dumpsters before dawn, that swoop down from the fence and dart through the gutters like comets?

What are they doing now? Nuzzling against pedestrians' ankles, mooching lunch leftovers off from school kids, getting pecked at by gliding starlings, basking in the sun in the middle of the road, exposing their fat guts, getting run over by bicycles, pressed flat like bookmark flowers? They'll get wiped out before I vanish. Except for those in Kyoto.

They are the genuine feral warriors. They have never forgotten to suspect mankind. They are expecting we will all get eradicated any day soon. And they will build a wild kingdom to complete, at last, the final feline plan for the Millennium City of Kyoto. Is this another curse of Kyoto? Do you think I'm joking?

They are both stupid creatures, cats and Z, but they'll have the last laugh. Z can't turn himself inside out, but he can turn his sweater inside out. And he will turn his back on us.

Skipping Kyoto with Z. Kyoto's thrilled at the thought. Kyoto knows the deal. They will escape the city together.

He will make it. She's been vaguely aware that he'll make it because of her. That's how the story always goes. And she will do it.

Kyoto hated Kyoto. Kyoto must have hated Kyoto, too.

Kyoto's parents were school trip refugees. They came to Kyoto when they were sixteen. In front of the Golden Pavilion, they pledged eternal love to one another. Two years later when they married, they disguised themselves as honeymooners and successfully broke across the border into Kyoto. Six days later, the wife found herself pregnant. The husband convinced himself her pregnancy was a conspiracy. He was shot by a Tower guard, making the conspiracy come true. The wife worked as a vendor at the betting booth at the Fushimi Race Track. Kyoto was born in the betting booth. Her mother passed away from postpartum shock.

Kyoto has no sweet memory of Kyoto. And now Kyoto will escape Kyoto with Z for good.

Z and Kyoto remain stuck to the Walls until sunset. The foreign music promises them everything that is not Kyoto. Now it's a mere whispering sound, but once they cross the Walls, they believed, the blasting sound will shake their bones, fill their empty stomachs.

They talk about the plan all night under the Bridge and make careful preparations.

The next morning, the two escape artists trot to Kyoto Station, hand in hand. The Tower still soars to the sky, the

Walls still stand thick and solid, and they are a little drowsy.

They have only one chance—to get on a Bullet Train, disguised as tourists. They must pay close attention to every possible thing so that the guards and the agents won't notice they're natives.

Kyoto is stunningly beautiful in the morning sunshine.

Z is dressed in the marvelously turned-over orange sweater. Perfect.

Only real tourists can buy train tickets, so they buy platform tickets permitted to natives.

By the time they reach the Bullet Train wicket, their platform tickets go all pulpy in their sweaty hands.

Thus Y quits his confession for the rest of the night.

V.

What happens to them afterward isn't much worth telling—actually it's a real drag to go through—but that'll ruin the whole story. So I must go on.

At the deck between cars of the Bullet Train, Z is pushing his face hard against the glass, stupefied. His hands are holding the hem of his orange sweater fast. Otherwise, his whole body starts quaking and clattering like a skeleton dancing in the dark.

I'm free, he murmurs to himself.

What a corny line. It sounds so unreal.

Z and Kyoto pass the ticketing gate all right. They make a naturally idiotic smile for the ticket examiners just like tourists always do in the Station.

Which car is your friends' car?

Number seven.

The trick is to utter such dialogue audible enough (but not too loud!), for no one would get on the train with a platform ticket. The two are here to pick up their friends.

They ascend the steps to the platform. Their Bullet Train will come in five minutes. All they have to do is to slip in. I bet their feeble hearts are beating fast! I bet they take such great pains not to let the other passengers hear their heartbeat!

The two stand on the platform. From now on, they must not meet the eyes of others. If they see their eyes, the others will know the two are natives. Z and Kyoto cuddle up together and fix their eyes on each other's pupils. They stare at each other so intensely that wrinkles gather on Z's forehead and Kyoto gets dizzy. There's a group of three old hags afar looking at the two, smiling and gabbing, Oh, what a sweet-looking couple.

One more minute and we are free. I look only in your eyes. Only myselves mirrored on your pupils.

The P.A. announces the train's approach. The bell rings.

The Bullet Train slides into the station yard. Z seizes a glimpse of it beyond Kyoto's shoulders. Kyoto sees the trains in his pupils. Almost there. Stay calm until the train stops and the door opens. That instant, Kyoto's gaze slightly deviates.

Inevitably he turns around, only too late. A man is running. Running toward them. The train stops. Kyoto grabs his arm and runs. It occurs to Z, Kyoto averted her eyes to avoid the eyes of the man far behind him.... Shoot, it was nothing he should have fretted about. If he hadn't turned around..., Z thinks vacantly, running to the door.

But it's too late. Too late.

The doors open. There's still some distance to the door. Z rushes ahead. He pulls her arm frantically. The man is fast, getting close. The bell rings again to announce the train's departure. Z clutches the door and throws himself in. At his violent tug, Kyoto's head bumps lightly against his chest. He closes his eyes. The door closes. His knees wobble. He exhales. His lashes tremble.

When Z opens his eyes again, Kyoto is not there. Through the glass window of the closed door, he sees Kyoto posing the same way as she listened to the music at the Walls the day before. She is pressing her widespread hands and left cheek against the glass window.

The train starts.

Kyoto sinks slowly, like the setting sun. He can't see her through the glass anymore, which is washed red all over. Through the bloodstained window, Z sees the man standing, his right arm limp, holding a weapon.

The train accelerates.

The wind gradually blows the blood on the glass behind him. The blood he will bury in oblivion some day. He looks away from the window and finds a red drop on his orange sweater.

He can't stop shaking.

Not because he's sad.

Not because he's scared of the new world coming to him.

Not because he rejoices in his freedom.

The train accelerates.

It will soon pass the Walls. The last drop of Kyoto on the glass slowly takes off quivering in the gale. He cries at that sight. But the tears will dry soon.

The Bullet Train thunders through the tunnel beyond the Walls.

And he sees the green cliffs and the sky as azure as her eyes. And nothing more.

This is it. This is it. This is the end of it!

Z has bolted.

You look disappointed. I bet you wanted to hear about my role in his escape, how I helped him and all. I don't know what I have to do with him. I don't even know what Z looks like. All I know is he has cleared the Walls. He made it because I told you this story. By telling you his story, I met him, knew him and set him free.

I wonder why he, not me. Why he escapes and I can't.

Oh, how much I loathe this city! This cursed city of Kyoto! Damned if I'd perish here. I should be breaking the bloody Walls. Ugh! Let me go, let me go!

Is this all I can do, to blab about some guy's escape? Isn't there any way for me? I wish I could erase this city. The Tower, the Walls, the River—everything. Altogether. Ha! What a good idea! And then, there would be only you and I left. Capital! Maybe I'm a genius. Ha ha ha ha! Vanish, Kyoto, vanish! Ha ha ha ha ha ha ha ha ha ha ha ha ha ha ha ha ha ha ha ha ha ha ha ha ha ha ha ha ha ha ha ha ha ha ha ha ha ha ha ha ha ha ha ha ha ha ha ha ha ha ha ha ha ha ha ha ha ha ha ha ha ha ha ha ha ha ha ha ha ha ha ha ha ha ha ha ha ha ha ha ha ha ha ha ha ha ha ha ha ha ha…

Y continues laughing. His dry laughter echoes in the underground cell. The echoes echo and disturb the darkness. Y keeps laughing. He laughs so hard that his bones clatter.

I assume Y has nothing left to talk about. Besides, another day dawns soon. My duty is to record Y's every single word, but I do not think it necessary to write down his endless laughter.

When I put down my pen, I find Y has vanished.

Ha ha.

Only his echoes remain.

marsupial, the lonely mammal

JULIET DITCHED ME. WHEN I WOKE UP, SHE WAS GONE. No message, no goodbye. She took our TV, our Playstation, our rice-cooker, our bike, my alarm clock, and my sunglasses. And she's left her dumb cat. She must've planned it for a while.

I know why she left. I've been unemployed for two months. I hadn't made any effort to find a job, but I was about to.

I stay in bed for three days and three nights, hoping Juliet will return. I've made her favorite tomato sandwich to keep in the fridge so that she can come home and eat it any time. Every evening, I get out of the bed to replace the soggy bread with some fresh slices. Juliet detests soggy bread. I give it to her stupid cat.

On the fourth day, I crawl out of bed and gobble down Juliet's sandwich. The tomato tastes bitter. I take bus 30 and tell the driver I've left my wallet in my office. She kicks me out. I walk to the job placement center, downtown.

They give me a sales job. I team up with Terry, an expert traveling saleskangaroo from Darwin.

We travel from door to door, selling trinkets. Terry talks to find out what ladies want, and I dig it out of his pouch. And ladies just love those plastic combs and synthetic leather gloves coming out of Terry's lukewarm pouch. Terry trains me and I help him with my able hands. We become buddies.

I tell him about Juliet one night at my place.

"I should've known she'd leave me. She'd always beat me up whenever I did anything wrong. This time she didn't. She'd been nice for two months. She even smiled at me."

Then I tell Terry how smart, nimble, diligent, and sometimes sweet Juliet was.

"She was too good for me."

"She'll be back." Terry taps on my back. Suddenly I feel terribly lonely. I look at Terry, who grins and slaps his belly.

"Come!"

I pillow my head on his belly. It is warm and soft, and smells of sunny grass. It reminds me of a huge bunny my mom made for me out of some worn-out blanket. The one that smelled like fresh piss steaming in the summer grass. This makes me weep for a second. I sniff into his fuzzy pouch. Juliet's shitty cat is napping inside. I squeeze it out before I screw my legs into his tummy. I put my arms around his neck and am about to doze off when the door bangs open and Juliet is standing there staring at us, my bottom sucked in Terry's pouch.

"What are you doing?" she barks.

I creep out of his pouch in silence. I introduce my co-worker to her, hoping Terry's kangarooness doesn't affect her judgment.

"Male marsupials don't have a pouch, you know," Juliet says. "I just wanted to see how you are doing. You've got such a capable partner. Nice. Goodbye." And before I say anything, she slams the door, which smashes my toe.

Terry's huddled up in the corner, scratching the edges of the half-stripped wallpaper. The cat is peeing on the carpet.

"So, you're a girl."

"I'm sorry. Thought you knew." And she hops out the door.

So I lose my job, again.

I loll in bed all day, dreaming of sunshine and fresh grass. The cat climbs onto my body and kneads my face. I ignore it and try to concentrate on my thoughts.

What will I tell her if she ever comes back?

Night falls.

I know neither of them will return. But it doesn't stop me from wishing.

a bus trip

THAT YEAR WAS ANOTHER UNFORTUNATE YEAR FOR the Chinese people. When panda bears started to invade the city of Xian, the capitalist TV cameras did not miss the bloody battle between the beasts and the human beings. People in front of the TV could tell right away which side was good or evil. The sight of the black-and-white funny-faced cubs randomly waving their plump plushy paws to cut the throats of the People's Liberation Army soldiers was simply too cute. People in front of the TV hated the Chinese. Chinese restaurants all over the world went out of business.

That spring, we took a sightseeing trip to Xian. That day, the sky was exceptionally clear for a spring day in Xian. The rain the day before had washed out the yellowish, powdery sand blown up by the constant northwestern wind from the Yellow River. The water on the ground formed innumerable streams, miniature yellow rivers, and turned into saffron mud in the meadows, where only peach blossoms did not lose their color of blush in the dusky mist.

The sightseeing bus left Hotel Victory at eight in the morning. The passengers were all foreigners. Our bus driver also served as the tour guide. No one understood his Shanxi dialect, which was all he could speak. We all agreed he was the handsomest Chinese man we'd ever seen. He was lean, thin-chested and had a sparse goatee. We were almost sure his hair had not been combed for a couple of weeks. A perpetual crease between his meager eyebrows emphasized his manliness. He never spoke except when we made stops at the sights. We assumed he was providing us with some information about the place. There was a clock above the windshield of the bus. Every time we made a stop, he put the clock forward to the departure time. We praised his cleverness.

The driver picked up his friend by the Great Gate of the old city. The city of Xian was surrounded by thick walls. Since the Panda Peril, the walls had been fortified, and sentries were posted. The Great Gate on the south wall had always been open, but now the gate was closed at five o'clock sharp because, for some unknown reason, the killer pandas were nocturnal. Not a cockroach was allowed to enter until five o'clock the next morning.

During the day, stalls of apple candies, bead accessories and sugar canes stood surrounding the gate. Pushcarts and bicycles came and went in a constant flow. The driver's friend made our bus stop outside the gate and bought a long thick stick of sugar cane. He sat next to the driver and never stopped talking. He spoke, chewing a mouthful of sugar cane, and even when he spat the cane fiber out of the front window and bit off another mouthful, he kept talking.

We started with the neighboring sightseeing spots, and then we had lunch at a famous dumpling restaurant, Restaurant Victory. They served pork dumplings only, and you had to order by the kilogram. We waited outside for a half hour. They wouldn't let anybody in until the entire dining room finished their dumplings. Then we were all seated around the round tables and dumplings were served in enameled bowls. It was recommended that we order one kilogram, which was equivalent to twenty-six dumplings. Each dumpling was the size of a professional wrestler's ear. The first five were delicious; the last three were torturous. We were not allowed to leave any in the bowls. We were not allowed to share them with one another.

After lunch, we drove to a rural area where all the important historic sites were. It was the highlight of the tour. After we threw up our lunch out of the windows, we were all ready and excited to see the Terracotta Warriors in the First Emperor Shih Hunangdi's Mausoleum. Thousands of life-size soldiers and horses formed up in ranks. Every soldier had a distinct face. Some had mustaches; some had their ears pierced.

Somebody said that if you found your own face among them, you would die within three days. Somebody else laughed at this stupid superstition. We saw mummies in a museum outside the mausoleum. They were naked, but the curators had put white cotton underpants on them. The Chinese are polite people. At the souvenir shop, we found tiny giant panda bears made of rabbit fur. We all bought some because as enlightened foreigners we supported endangered species.

On our way back to the old city, our bus broke down in the middle of an abandoned village. We all panicked. Sunset was approaching, and we thought we heard rustling in the bamboo woods behind the ruined farmhouses. Our driver turned and threw a couple of sharp words at us. We shut up. He gave us some commands and grabbed a small hammer and a roll of adhesive tape and got out of the bus. We all sighed in despair because even a hard-boiled man like our driver had no chance to repair a vehicle with Scotch tape. Now through the evergreen bamboo, we could see the adorable, smiley eyes of blood-hungry beasts sparkling here and there.

Just as we gave a shrill cry, our driver came back into the bus and started the engine. We were all awed by his dexterity and praised him as a man amongst men.

Our driver-cum-guide gunned the bus spewing up clouds of yellow dust under the squeaky wheels, following the trace of sugar cane spit onto the ground. The moment we dashed into the Great Gate, the five o'clock bell rang. When our group broke up at the foot of the bell tower in front of the gate, we noticed we were missing somebody.

It was the Hoosier businessman who had laughed at the curse of the Terracotta Warriors. We whispered to each other that he must've seen his own face among the ancient mud soldiers. He must have been silently chopped up by a panda bear in the ruined village. We were glad we hadn't died.

At the foot of the bell tower, a boy was scratching the yellow earth with his bare hands. A Canadian schoolteacher asked him in Mandarin what he was doing.

He was digging a grave to bury his father who had been killed by a killer panda. His father was a brave soldier. The only remains of his father was his Adam's apple bone. The boy kept scratching the dirt, staring down at the ground with his lips closed tight. The hole was shallow, but it was enough for one Adam's apple bone. When he finished the burial, a teardrop fell on the ground. A sprout stuck out of the wet yellow earth. It grew fast in front of our eyes, and then a violet poppy-like flower came into blossom. Our brave driver-cum-guide sighed and lit a cigarette. Purple smoke rose from its tip. When it touched the sweet petals, the flower shrank, quickly fading to stinky beige, and its stem drooped.

octavia

I AM DREAMING. I AM ON A ROCK TOWER IN THE DESERT. Its top is flat and wide enough for two, so a woman and I are having tea sitting on flat cushions there. I cannot see the ground because the dust obscures the depth. But I judge it to be three thousand feet below us at least. The sun is shining. The air is dry and clear. The sunbeams sting my eyes. I cannot see the woman's face. It's completely dark. I ask her to switch seats. She says yes. So we stand up. Stones drop off the cliff. They sound like kitten bells. The sound never ceases. I feel a little dizzy. We put our backs tightly together and carefully shift over toward each other's side. I hear myself saying, slowly, slowly, don't look down. She does. She slips. I see her slowly fall into the abyss. So slowly that I could catch her, but I cannot. She falls with her head up, eyes wide open, and arms spread. Her face, the face I now see, shows no fear. There is no sound but bells rolling down the cliff. I tell myself this is a dream, I am dreaming.

Goodness, it *was* a dream! I let out a big sigh and rise from the bed. I've had many nightmares where I myself freefall, but they don't scare me as much as watching another person falling—I've never imagined this could be such a frightening, entirely another point of view. My silk pajama shirt sticks to my chest. Pressing my hands under my arms, I look aside and find Etsuko is out of bed. She must be preparing lunch; it is eleven thirty already. I overslept. I drag myself out of the bed to change clothes.

My name is Kazuo Harada. I'm ~~a literary hack~~ an emerging young popular novelist. I'm enjoying my early thirties with my beautiful wife Etsuko and our loyal spaniel Tin-Tin. I've been successful enough in my writing career to buy an agreeable 3 bedroom house with a small garden in the suburb. Today is November 13th, the deadline for my 25-page short story for *Dream City Review*, the national best-selling entertainment magazine. AND I HAVEN'T WRITTEN A PAGE YET, words silently scream in uppercase. My eyes are vacuumed onto the blank sheets of paper scattered over my oak writing desk.

"Honey, Mr. Fujita is at the door!" Etsuko yells from downstairs.

"Tell him to come later in the evening!" If Fujita weren't my editor, I would just kick his ass out. I shout back wishing there was a freshly finished piece of fiction underneath the pile of paper, but before I can finish my words, *whump-smash*, and my loving wife's shrill cry alarms me.

"Etsuko!" I rush downstairs calling my sweetheart's name. I know Fujita has been coveting her for years, I knew it! That swine! At the living room door, I find the one-eyed editor Fujita is fiercely clutching Etsuko's wrists in one hand and pulling her hair back in the other.

"Mr. Harada, you must've finished your story, huh? How many times have I postponed your deadline? You pulp hacks think editors are wimps. Losers. Whining and begging at your feet for your million-dollar manuscripts, just because they can't write themselves. Yes! I knew it! Now, could you hand me your manuscript? Your blood, tears, and sweat? Please? It must be another masterpiece since you've spent so much time on it? Right, Mr. Harada? So where's your precious manuscript? Poor Fujita's been waiting for it. For weeks. You've promised. So give it to me today. Now!—But it can't be possible that … you haven't … after all this? Oh, I'm sorry… Oh no. Ooh…. Then you know what happens to your beautiful wife," says Fujita and licks his thick greedy lips.

"Fujita, you bastard!" I grind my teeth.

Fujita laughs, "Oh, you call me whatever you like. Ha ha. Me, a poor little editor desperate for another el cheapo manuscript!"

"My darling," Etsuko cries at me, "Please go! He'll lock you up in the publisher's office again. Don't worry about me. Run!"

Clacking his tongue, Fujita calls my graceful wife *bitch*.

He stretches out his long hairy arm to grab my neck while holding my love's long hair in the other hand. She cries for pain but still keeps shouting, "Go…darling. Run!"

I escape from Fujita's reach and run to the kitchen window. Tears run down my cheeks.

"Forgive me, Etsuko. I shall return with a masterpiece to save you from that stinker. Wait till I come back, honey. Adios!" and I jump off the window.

My feet are cold. They hurt. I've left home barefoot. I'm smoking on a pedestrian bridge over a boulevard. It's a few miles away from home. I'm tired from running. I put my elbows on the railing to rest my chin and view the busy road.

I think of this morning's dream. I was twenty in the dream. What was I like thirteen years ago? A hot and sour uproar runs through me whenever I reminisce about that period. I was haughty, fierce, desperate, hopeful, poor and lonesome. Yes, I secluded myself in my messy four-and-a-half-tatami-matted nook, bursting with ambition, squeezed by anxiety, yet my hands were empty. I was a hungry beast refusing to feast. I wasted my time and talent, not knowing what they really meant. It was the most dazzling moment of my life, and the most painful and pitiful. I would never go back to that age however precious and sweet it was.

I hear a sound coming up the bridge steps. It's a girl speaking to someone. A chipper laughter and trotting footsteps approach. A fluffy butterfly ribbon in robin's-egg-blue pops out at the end of the bridge, then a girl's face. She is busy talking to someone hidden behind her and doesn't notice me. Her speech still carries a hint of baby talk. Finding me, she stops talking at the top of the steps. The late autumn sun shines tenderly upon her marshmallow face as she trots straight to me.

She's dressed in a lavender cotton flannel dress. It is old fashioned with a puffy skirt over lacy petticoats and a fringed muslin sash. Pearl-shaped buttons line up in a row under the lace-trimmed collar. She wears white tights and a pair of white enamel Mary Janes. The surface of her fine dark hair shines sheer chestnut in the sun all the way to her shoulder blades. Finally I notice her pair of pink mittens with red pompons.

She looks up at me and gives a curious smile.
"Hello."
"Hello," I reply. "How are you?"
"My name is Yuko. What is your name, Daddy?"
I tell her my name.
"How do you do?" She bobs like a rabbit in the grass.

I say that I thought she was with a friend. With a contented smile she says she is and runs behind me to the other side.

The sun shines upon her back now. She stretches out her arm to indicate the dark figure at her feet in the exact same shape and pose as herself.

"This is my best friend, Octavia."

"Why, it's your—" *sh*wallowing the last word at the top of my throat, I faintly smile down. "Hello, Octavia."

"Octavia says, *How do you do?*" says Yuko and gives her bunny bow again; Octavia bows to me simultaneously. "She's a little bit shy"—those are Yuko's words.

I don't know what to say. I'm not a good baby-sitter at all. Small children baffle me. They drain my energy. I don't care about them very much. While I lean against the railing, puzzled, Yuko squats and gazes at my feet with her small mouth open.

"Is it your barefoot day today, Daddy?" She sounds bewildered.

"No, I didn't have time to put on my shoes," I answer indifferently.

"That's too bad. They are crying."

"I know."

Yuko pulls her pink pompon mittens off her hands and offers them to me without a word. I shake my head, hoping she will leave me alone. But she pushes them hard against my belly until I give in. I sit at the foot of the railing and pretend to put them on. They magically stretch and their wrists reach my ankles. I look at my feet; they look like huge monkey feet. The mittens are too tight but I feel better.

"Now they are happy," Yuko laughs.

"Thank you."

"It's Octavia's idea." Yuko seems proud to say so.

"Thank you, Octavia." I bow to the ground.

"Heh." Yuko looks up at me as Octavia timidly pulls her head back.

We three start to walk together to the east. My mitten thumbs flip-flop as I walk. I have to watch my feet not to step on them. Yuko is busy talking to Octavia who is walking ahead of us. The sun puts many folds on Octavia as we go down the bridge steps.

"Are you listening, Daddy?"

"Yes, yes, I am, Yuko."

"Are you drowsy?"

"No, no, Octavia."

"We're hungry!" When she abruptly says so, I find myself hungry too, so we decide to go to the Old Town to share a giant strawberry parfait at Ichigoya.

"People must have a great deal of trouble telling you from Octavia," I say to Yuko just to avoid silence while waiting for the traffic signal to change. A sudden seriousness comes over Yuko's round face. She draws her face close to mine as I bend to listen to her.

"It is really, very difficult. But I'll tell you a secret. Guess what." She looks around to make sure nobody else is listening to us and tiptoes to whisper into my ear. Her cheeks smell like a kitten in the sun. Yuko spreads out her right palm in front of my face.

"Octavia holds chopsticks in the other hand!"

"…Wow."

That's all I can say.

I'm sure my whole energy would ebb away by the end of the day if I kept company with this young lady. The signal turns green.

Yuko calls her friend's name and they skip across the street together. I feebly walk behind them.

"See? Octavia can run faster than me," Yuko says, panting after skipping. "She does everything better than me. I'm so clumsy."

But everyone likes Yuko—I think I hear some girl saying—*Yuko is honest and kind. She has many, many friends. I have no friend but Yuko.*

Then she becomes shy and silent again.

I find Yuko clumsy indeed. She clenches her spoon in her fist and levers it up, so every other scoop of her parfait flips away somewhere else from her small (but opened as large as possible) mouth. She doesn't care. Octavia catches all she misses. Yuko keeps talking while eating. She is trying to tell me all the adventures she and Octavia went through though I cannot catch most of them, for she speaks with her mouth full. I pull out my handkerchief from my pants' pocket and wipe the cream off her cheeks and dress. Yuko narrows her eyes and purrs.

"You must leave the last strawberry for me," I warn Yuko since I haven't had any strawberries yet. Nevertheless she gives it to Octavia. They both lick their lips with contentment. I drop my shoulders. I love strawberries. I look at the girls resentfully as they tom-tom their tummies.

We go outside. Tall gingko trees along the streets are at their golden peak. Yuko and Octavia play hide-and-seek along the trees. Leaves keep falling down upon me, Yuko and Octavia. Two Russian wolfhounds, one black and the other white, led by an elderly woman, are startled by us. The white one barks at Yuko and the dark one at Octavia. We all laugh.

Octavia grows taller and thinner. My feet get colder in the pink pompon mittens. Street lamps turn on one by one.

Yuko points at them and shouts, "Don't they look like cinnamon candies? See, Octavia!"

As Yuko runs zigzag between streetlights, many Octavias in various heights and shades circle around Yuko.

I find a telephone box. While I dial home, Yuko pushes her face against the glass to make a piggy face. Octavia patiently stands behind her.

"Is it you, my darling? Thank goodness!" My faithful wife's voice sounds so bright that I know right away she is alright.

"Are you okay, Etsuko? I'm sorry I left you."

"I'm fine, dear."

"How's Fujita?"

"He's melted."

I beg her pardon.

"I threw a bottle of salt at him and he melted away."

So that's what that slug really was after all.

"I'm coming home soon, honey."

"Yes. I love you." I hear sobs in her voice.

I feel like crying, too.

Now I come out of the telephone box and look at the girls.

"It's time to go home, girls. I'll walk you home. Where do you live?"

Yuko's face turns pitiful all at once. Her chin is drawn to her chest, her cheeks become puffy and her eyes grow larger. She grabs her dress sash in her hands and stares down at Octavia. As if they had their own secret to discuss.

She looks in my eyes and says, "We don't have a home."

A big teardrop comes out of her right eye. Another big drop comes out of Octavia's left eye. They both hold their eyes as wide open as possible at me.

"We don't have a family." Yuko sounds almost angry. She grabs the hem of my sweater, watching the ground. I see four dimples on her fist.

"We're alone. Just me and Octavia."

I look at her again, this time more closely. She wears a nice dress, but it is shabby. Its sleeves are almost threadbare at the elbows. Her hair hasn't been combed for days apparently. Many parts of her hem laces are torn. Her fingers are red and thick from frostbite.

With her lips poked out, Yuko looks like a peevish duckling. And her only friend Octavia is diminishing into the twilight. I hurry them under the street lamp before they lose each other.

I kneel and put my hands on her shoulders.

"Do you want to come home with me?"

"We don't have a home." The two girls let go of their hands from my sweater.

"I mean, do you want to live with us? Do you want to become me and my wife's family?"

She casts a pouty glance up at me.

"Do you want us to?"

I nod. The two hold my sweater again.

"*Promise?*" Now this is from both girls.

"Of course, I promise."

The next moment, they are jumping and dancing like twin little monkeys. They run in circles around me, cheering.

Then we walk home together holding hands.

They are so excited that I have to tell them to calm down again and again.

We see our house's light from afar. My dearest wife must be preparing dinner. As we approach our home, we sing together, swinging arms:

Let's go home hand in hand
Our house's light is brightest
and warmest. Let's go home

"I'm home, Etsuko!" I ring the door

—and I woke up
Grabbing the damp, flat futon, I raised myself. The wall clock read 4:59. It was right after dawn. Sparrows were tweeting. A milkman rode off ringing the bicycle bell. I scratched my bony

back underneath my sweaty T-shirt. The room smelled of the socks I had hung the night before on the rope across the room. A couple of mosquitoes were buzzing around the back of my neck. I saw another one drowned in some flat beer left in an unclean glass on the last evening's newspaper. The window screen must have a hole. The night lamp was on. I had fallen asleep reading a book. Underwear, books, magazines, plastic bags, cans and other unidentifiable items scattered all over around my worn-out futon. I could hardly see the tatami floor. The August sun was already burning hot at dawn. My forehead was getting oily. Another day had come.

I found myself in my messy four-and-a-half-tatami-matted nook. I was very thirsty, but too dazzled to know what to do. It was now. It took me a while to realize. I was twenty years old. And I was alone.

I tried to breathe deep and slow. I turned my head around and found a dark shape of a young man looking at me on the west wall. I raised my right hand to greet my friend; he raised his left hand no later.

Hello, I said, but my friend was shy.
I named him Dmitry.

a goldfish galaxy

Xiphias unlocked the apartment door, Aurora between his arms, cornering her as they entered the living room through the foyer. When the light turned on, Aurora gasped at the large convex mirror over the golden fireplace. The hemisphere on the wall sucked the world into the miniature left-hand system, startling every visitor. Xiphias kissed Aurora … a second time … carefully and lightly…. He placed his hand on her rib cage to measure the curvature. Aurora let out a faint Champagne sigh…. Another kiss, a short, but more pressing one. Her eyes were moist—her irides had gained a gold sheen—whether this aberration was nocturnal or amorous, he did not know.

Xiphias's apartment was on the tenth floor, overlooking the dense growth of the park trees across the boulevard. There wasn't any curtain or blind in the living room. The tall windows reflected the two entranced by each other, blinding themselves to the stellar night outside.

What shall we do? Xiphias asked, intending to be rhetorical, pretending to abandon the initiative to the captive.

I don't know.... Aurora replied, giving up the imaginary dominance. The two kissed.... This lasted for a while....

...They were ready to seat themselves in the long sofa in the center of the living room. It was blue and made of glazed leather. Xiphias strategically placed her sideways, locking her stretched knees between his herringboned legs—one bent on the sofa and the other pegged on the floor. Aurora shivered on the cold leather. A giggle bubbled up and she submitted herself to the hair-raising touch of the blue leather... her back revolute, revealing the skin behind her ear.... A mule sandal clanked off on the floor.

Before she closed her eyes as Xiphias bent over her, Aurora beheld a goldfish bowl on the side table within her arm's reach. She made an evanescent mental note not to knock it over.... She caught a glimpse of the two fish, black and red, levitating inside the glass orb before she closed her eyes....

The red goldfish was an oranda—an overdressed voluptuous with a heaped coiffure and a flaring train of veil tail. The black one was a telescope, a black moor, perpetually goggling at its flashy companion.... The two floated, undulated, crossed over, and flickered.... Veils of light unfolded and refolded, asterisms twinkling across the dark planisphere behind his eyelids. The heat, the odor of the leather, and the rustles of the silk skirt were unbearable. Xiphias began to undo her blouse's pearl buttons; Aurora followed his lead, redoing them, her nimble fingers always interfering with his unbuttoning hands.... They played the game of tag over the row of seven buttons several times back and forth until the male perseverance almost conquered the hills, but the troop changed its course midway—instead of advancing further south, it flew to the dark side of the moon, under the arching spine, snapping the hook, breaking the ground rules altogether. The celestial body now supine in the deep blue froze for a moment, caught by surprise, the pearly constellation aligned perfectly still. Then the body began to wriggle.... Aurora's pink skirt twisted halfway up, which he did not miss. Xiphias slid his hot palm above her cold knee.... Aurora moaned faintly.

In the night sky, the moon was new, letting the galaxy sparkle. The black telescope was Newtonian, pudgy and solid, like a metal model of some imaginary organ, with two tubes sticking out from the orb. Inside the reflection telescope, time glided on, stars glimmered, constellations traversed, goldfish spacewalked. The open secret inside the telescope was that it kept the whole of the universe.... But a mere revolution of heavenly spheres did not reveal all the cosmographic mysteries to the naked eye in Isfahan. The legs must be used.... The man must travel to the lower extremity of Arabia to complete his uranometry, the book of fixed stars. Dark nebulae must be groped, dwarf galaxies sucked, cosmos outlined, heavenly bodies delineated. The sidereal messenger was ascending into the thin air, guided by the Maghrebi and Arabian ox … panting … gasping … across the ecliptic and *Via Lectea*. It was another foggy day on the Table Mountain covered with the dossal. Mensa was behind a cloud, always blurry. Hence the inquisition was postponed; the survey was prolonged; the octant was protracted. And the angle was measured according to the mathematical principles.... There were 265 men when the vessels left Sanlúcar. Fish dolphins raced with the dashing vessels. As soon as sailors dipped their rods, swordfish rambled, bit the baits, but slipped away from their grip, flipping in the air, wet scales glistening for a sidereal second, the slippage would later turn out a fatal lag.... Brine splashed on the young sailor's ruddy face.

He tried his lithe rod again. There were fewer and fewer men left onboard. It was getting dark. One vessel had disappeared. Where they were heading was beyond his ken. He felt uneasy. It wasn't seasickness. Yet there was no way going back. The vitrified orb seduced: *primus circumdidisti me*. He felt a tug, a jerk, *pull, pull, pull!* Or push? Or let it swim? He flapped. A fin slashed out of the blue current. The auros dorsum resplending, the dorado slowly emerged upright from the water, like a bronze falchion. Once in the air, the sheer weight of the dorado almost broke the pole. The fish knocked itself against the broadside several times before the ruddy-faced sailor embraced its golden body, and it was quickly turning lifeless in his arms … the auros gleam fading away so fast by the miraculous trick of optics that the young sailor almost wept, the swelled spindle becoming cavernous by the second, going flaccid, on the wane. The sailor helplessly watched its corneae growing murky…. It was completely dark now. Nebulae were surfacing from the deep space. Ephémérides announced the coming of fall. The golden fish went west, having turned roily gray. Another burial at sea…. Fewer men were left. Only 17 in the end…. The celestial discharge embellished the night of the starry austral heaven. Feeling sorry won't bring time back…. The Galaxy, the spilt milk in the night sky, remained remote in the punchbowl. The orb sat there still. The milk was never spilt to begin with. The swordfish lay there limp, alone.

On the southern tip of Arabia, Al Sufi sighed at the nebula. All the while he was walking at night he only gazed upward because the stellar landscape kept changing as they walked. He didn't want to miss any. His servant had kept an eye on the direction they were heading. Now Al Sufi looked forward for the first time in months and there was the ocean. Cold and blue. *Only if I had a boat!* The Yemeni fishermen were already sailing out in the dark.

chick sexing school, or how our dead grandfather summoned me and my brother to japan

It was right after our grandfather died when my brother George suddenly started to resemble him. To be precise, George started to look like the portrait of Grandpa.

I never met my mother's father, Grandpa Taketora, while he was alive. Or dead, for that matter. I like to pretend, at least, he was in his coffin, pale and all wrinkled up when I finally saw his face in December 1959. I could tell you details as if I had been at the wake, like, how his gray hair sticking out of his nostrils bothered me; the tails of his eyebrows were almost touching his closed eyelashes. He was so big for a

Japanese man of his age that the undertakers had to bend his knees to fit him into an extra-large coffin.

But this is not true. I couldn't see his real face, dead or alive. When I met Grandpa at last, he wasn't Matsuda Taketora any more. He had been given a protracted, incomprehensible posthumous Buddhist name. He had been cremated, put into a ceramic urn, and placed in his family grave on a hill that commands the Omura Bay.

I had never seen Grandpa Taketora's photograph, either. All I had seen was his oil portrait, which still hangs in our living room. He is in his mid-thirties in the portrait. I must admit he is quite handsome. There he stands, flat against the velvety, gloomy background. He is lean and tall, wearing the Japanese Imperial Army's uniform, which doesn't exist on the earth any more, thank Goodness. Five decorations on his chest dully gleam in ocher. Grandpa Taketora's prominent features are his wise looking forehead, lean, lofty nose, and the stubborn-looking thick black eyebrows above gold-rimmed round spectacles on his long, clean-shaven face. My mother doesn't look like him at all. She is a round-faced, button-nosed, short-limbed woman.

I regret that I didn't benefit from atavism. Though I inherited none of my maternal side's features, I had been his favorite, because I was his first grandchild.

My parents married without telling Grandpa Taketora. Since then, Grandpa Taketora had never sent her a word, even a New Year's card. The official excuse was that he could not admit that Ma had chosen to stay in America and marry Pa, a *nisei*, an American born, "a degenerated Japanese"—Grandpa might say—who dared to volunteer to fight against his own people in the war. This is not true, by the way. Pa fought against the Germans in Europe. I think Grandpa had been simply difficult because his daughter didn't come back to him. He insisted that my mother's stay in America with her aunt was temporary, but technically speaking, she wasn't his daughter anymore.

My mother's mother passed away around 1920, leaving her and her three older siblings. Her father, Grandpa Taketora, was in service in Siberia and had no idea when he could come home. The Reds were so stubborn in Siberia. He had to give up his children to his relatives' care. Three relatives in Japan looked after the three older children, and my mother was sent to her aunt Satoko in San Francisco. Auntie Satoko, who had divorced an Irish-American man, adopted Ma right away before the Anti-Japanese Immigration Law passed in 1924. This made it difficult for Ma to go back to Japan. Although Ma admits that she hoped to remain in America for her own interest, it was not only her fault that she did not return.

As California became a difficult place to live for the Japanese, Auntie Satoko moved to Utah with Ma. I know they moved a couple of more times afterwards, but from then up until I was born, their stories suddenly get obscure. I don't want to ask what they don't want to talk about, so they still remain obscure. All I know is that Ma met Pa before he went to Europe, and after he came back, they moved to Tacoma, where we live now.

Grandpa didn't know that my brother and I had been born until the war was over. I was two and my brother one when Grandpa learned that Japan had lost the war against America but he had gained two grandchildren in America. Though it took him five more years to accept us, that's when he sent his portrait to his daughter. My mother remembered the portrait well. It had been hung on his drawing room wall, when she was little, over the leather chair where Grandpa sat and smoked while waiting for his patients. In the spring of 1950, when Ma tore open the brown parcel paper and saw the ocher medals revealed, she realized right away that it was her father's sign that he would permit her marriage, her way of life, and accept the two of us as his grandchildren. She has treasured the portrait ever since, and it will be my job to carry along the portrait in the future, because my mother always tells me that my mere existence regained our ties to the extended family.

We grew up hearing stories of Grandpa Taketora from Ma and Auntie Satoko.

He was six foot four and could lift three hundred pounds. He swam across the Omura Bay when he was twelve. When he was a teenager, he used to dunk himself into the Nono River at five every morning, snow or rain, dredging the water for sweetwater clams for his family's breakfast. He won a national scholarship to study medicine at an Imperial University. He knew more than four thousand Chinese characters. He won two medals in the First World War and three in the Siberian Dispatch. But when we asked Ma and Auntie Satoko how he acquired those ocher medals, nobody knew. Ma and Auntie Satoko would assure me, whenever I asked, that Grandpa Taketora was an army surgeon, so he got the medals for saving people's lives, not for killing them. I sort of bought it, but my brother George didn't.

He didn't say he didn't believe their stories, but I knew he suspected our Grandpa had killed at least a couple of pre-Nazi Germans and Red partisans in his years of service.

Poor Germans and Russians, they had to play the role of expendable extras in our family epic. Grandpa Taketora was a mythic hero. All the more so for his bodily absence and his portraited presence in our house.

Ever since he had sent us the portrait, Grandpa Taketora kept writing to us until he was hospitalized for cancer of the larynx. A few lines were devoted to his life in Omura: not only did he work in his clinic, he was the head of the municipal health center; we heard about vaccinations and nutrition education in his small town. His letters gave me an impression that Japan had a long way to go to improve its public hygiene.

I learned things like this Japanese superstition: if you get poisoned by *fugu*, the poisonous blowfish, the Japanese will bury you alive with your head sticking out of the earth like a neglected winter squash. Grandpa had blowfish-poisoned patients a couple of times a year. Usually a stomach pump would save them, but once this poor middle-aged man, who illegally cooked blowfish that he fished himself, came too late to his clinic because he had been left half buried in the dirt for half the day.

Besides his life in Japan, Grandpa spent many lines describing what he wanted George and me to become. That was the cream of his letters. He sounded quite authoritative, like any mythic hero. George would be a doctor naturally, Grandpa Taketora asserted, and he had planned my life according to the years left in his life. He wanted me to do as much as his old-fashioned imagination allowed a woman to do while he was still alive. After I finished my compulsory education, I would marry a good Japanese man on my sixteenth birthday (the legal age for a woman to marry in Japan) and bear his great-grandchild in nine months sharp. He would be seventy-eight by then. He would die, he wrote again and again, after he saw his first great-grandchild. He always wrote that he could wait only until I became sixteen.

Every time I thought of Grandpa's obsession, an imaginary scene came into my mind—he would pass away at the peak of his delight, lying spread-eagled on the runway, upon seeing me descending the steps from the transpacific airplane, landing on his soil with my newborn baby in my arms. "Grandpa! Grandpa!" My parents, George, and I would run up to him and jolt him, but his contented smile would be peacefully fixed on his long face. We would shoulder him back to the airport terminal, each of us holding a limb, since he was so big. I wouldn't be able to hold my baby in my arms while I'd support Grandpa's limb, so my baby would be laid on its belly on Grandpa's belly. Then I'd suddenly come back to reality, asking myself, where is the baby's father, where is my husband? He should be carrying my baby while I am taking part in the triumphant yet tragic end of our hero. Then I would finally realize how impossible the first premise of the scene was. How could I get married at sixteen? With whom? Can I scream?

In his letters, he always counted the years he had to wait. Every letter was a countdown. It sounded as if he couldn't wait for his last day. I have felt sorry for Grandpa because I have known all along that his dream wouldn't come true. When I was ten, my dream was to become a head keeper of a zoo or an ostrich breeder.

Even as a ten-year-old, I was aware that having a baby at the age of sixteen would be a great obstacle to my future career. My parents had their own expectations for me and George, but marrying me off at sixteen was not one of them. But Grandpa's countdown letters kept coming.

The letters were written in Japanese mixed with many knotty Chinese characters I had never seen. Even after Ma read them aloud to us, we needed some words rephrased or interpreted. Sometimes all of us got lost in the labyrinth of his old-fashioned Eastern rhetoric.

And today, I am still sorry and confused because he did wait until I became sixteen. He died a month before my seventeenth birthday. Long enough to have a baby. Was he serious about his plans? If so, what could I have done for him instead of just feeling guilty and telling him nothing?

Looking back on my past, I was always more concerned about my career than romance. I became acquainted with my first uninspiring date when I was fourteen while I acquired my first chickens at the age of ten. Aspiring to be a top ostrich breeder, it was natural that I started with a smaller kind. I bought the chicks from the old Mexican man who used to bring chicks in baskets to our grade school. He was trying to sell chickens to school kids. Kids liked to pat the creatures, but the chicks weren't selling well. Bringing a chick back home was a different story from buying marbles on our way home from school. There were two baskets of chicks: one for hens and one for roosters. He sold a hen for a quarter and a cock for a nickel. He would appear one or two times a month and squat at the edge of the yard near the school entrance, smoking a long Chinese pipe. His chickens were busy chirping and pushing each other about. Sometimes they were so loud they sounded like rain falling on a tin roof. Their feathers were different shades of chicken yellow: some were almost creamy white and some were sunny yellow, and there was every possible shade in between. Before Easter break every year, his chickens were dyed pastel with food colors. Orange chickens, pink chickens, blue chickens. Once Easter was over, the chickens would go back to the normal gradations between ivory and yellow.

The first time I touched the chickens, brushing against the flock of them squeezed in the basket, I wish I could tell you, *Electricity thundered from the tips of my fingers through my spine and limbs and I felt my hair bristle up; and right away I realized that it was a predestined encounter—me and chickens.* But this is not true. Stroking their feathers, I actually chuckled. The surface of the fidgeting bunch of warm down tickled me. Then the Mexican man grabbed one chicken and held it out to me. I offered my palms side by side. He put the chicken on my palms. I curved my palms and shaped two hemispheres to form a round cage for the chicken. The interior of my hand cage felt a scurrying sunny ball of fur, and I was still chuckling, feeling lemon-yellow airy feathers filling me up and warming me up. I put the chicken back into the girl basket and hurried home to persuade Ma and Pa.

This is how I obtained my first three chicks and how I got into the whole business about chickens. Before they were large enough to stay outside, they lived in our room. I kept them in a worn-out cardboard box. I held them in the round cage of my palms, one by one in turn. I could do it all day.

I called my chickens Chicken-One, Chicken-Two and Chicken-Three, because as much as the feeling of those little yellow down balls in my hand, I liked the sound of "chicken" to my ears. The jumpy syllable followed by the comforting grounding of a nasal sound pleased my tongue.

Chicken, Chicken, Chicken.

I kept repeating their names while I played with them. Chicken-One, Chicken-Two, Chicken-Three. I was very happy. Until my mother found a need to intervene between me and my chickens. She didn't find Chicken an aesthetic name for chickens. She thought I was playing the role of an oppressive warden with my chickens.

"Eleanor, don't call your pets by numbers," she said. "They are not prisoners. They are your friends, Eleanor. Give them nice names."

I tried, but I had to tell her I couldn't find any more suitable name than Chicken for them.

"Okay," Ma said nonchalantly. "Let me name them for you."

Then, I realized she had been waiting for this moment, but it was too late to stop her. She had had their names in her mind already. She named Chicken-One, the white girl chick, Tosca, Chicken-Two, the only boy, Tristan, and Chicken-Three, the yellowish girl chick, Isolde. Before I knew it, it became our family rule to name chickens something like Aida and Ladames, Carmen and Don Jose, Rodolpho and Mimi, and Papageno and Papagena.

My mother always wanted to become an opera singer. That's why she didn't want to go back to Japan even after Grandpa Taketora came back from Siberia. She wanted to go to a music school in San Francisco. But soon for various reasons it turned out too difficult for her to pursue her dream. I think it was a good idea that she gave up the prima donna thing because, even if she had made it, what roles could she play as a prima? Not much choice. The frustrated Chinese princess who kills men and the neglected Japanese geisha who kills herself. That sounds like a morbid prima-donna life.

My love for chickens caused me some hardships, too. I was so much into my three chickens that I couldn't eat any kind of poultry anymore. At the dinner table, I would poke at the bumps of chicken skin with my fork, thinking of death and my chickens, until tears welled up in my eyes. This habit drove my parents crazy. The fuss snowballed as my thing infected George, the more sensitive one. We wept in chorus, poking the plump poultry in pity for the poor poussin together until we were sent to bed in disgrace.

This symptom lasted for three months until I found twin baby owls in the woods in the park. Two fat piles of gray down were cuddling together at the base of an oak tree. They must have fallen from their nest. They were too little to fly.

I couldn't keep them as pets. Ambitious as I was, skipping from chicks to raptors was a leap too sudden. I asked Ma for help. She found a veterinarian in Forrest Creek who took care of injured big birds. We brought the baby owls to his clinic, which was full of big falcons, old kites, and grown-up owls, all sick and hurt. They were motionless and sullen in the cages. I smelled their wounds and diseases. I felt the air vibrating with shame, shame for their disgraceful scars.

"Let's see. Hmm. The birdies are quite meek!"

Dr. Cheyenne peeped into the box of owls we put on the counter. The baby owls were still stuck together like Siamese twins.

"How come they are so down?" the doctor cheerfully said, rubbing his hands. "They are not hurt or anything. I wonder if they are hungry. Let's see."

He opened the maple wood drawer under the counter in a businesslike manner. Standing behind Dr. Cheyenne, the contents of the drawer jumped at my eyes. It was full of fluffy yellow things. They were freshly dead chickens. There were about thirty of them, cleanly dead, lying in the drawer, riveting my eyes. Seeing my paralyzed face, Ma's eyes reflected great regret. She must have thought, *oh no, this is the last blow; Eleanor won't eat chicken for the rest of her life; what should I do with the chicken left in the icebox?*

The doctor pinched out two chicken corpses, and put them under the owls' noses. The birds squeezed against each other even tighter. They didn't seem to understand the furry balls were their lunch. Dr. Cheyenne sniffed at this sight, whipped a knife out of his laboratory coat, and started to dress the tiny chickens. This made me weep. Ma touched my shoulders, but she was also amazed at my stupidity. The chickens didn't bleed. The doctor nimbly peeled the feathers and skin off, and I saw the flesh of the tiny chicken breasts, about the size of my thumb, but otherwise the same fresh, skinned chicken meat I had seen at the market. I don't remember other details. I don't recall whether the owls ate the meat or not. I was devastated, yet the image of the tiny pink chicken breast led me to come to terms with the relationship between man and chicken. The fragile chicken, cute to look at, nice to play with, good to eat. From that day, I resumed eating poultry. I could chew and swallow chicken again.

Meanwhile, my three chickens, Tosca, Tristan, and Isolde, had passed the cutest phase of their life and became ugly, angry adolescents. Their cream feathers were mixed with yellow down; their little cockscombs didn't match their baby faces.

In short, they looked like vertically stretched chickens somebody created by mistake.

And poor Isolde, she turned out to be a rooster!

The old Mexican man had told me she was a girl! Of course, I waited for him to reappear in front of the school and complained to him. He promptly apologized for his mistake. To my surprise, this kind of mistake would happen sometimes, he said, and gave me a newborn girl chicken, and a boy chicken in addition. He put a red rubber band around the girl chick's leg. I timidly asked him if I had to return Isolde to him. He waved his hands and shook his head, repeating, *no, no*. So I was very happy, getting two more chicks for free. I named them Romeo and Juliet on my way home. Romeo was a rooster and Juliet was a hen.

Two years passed. Carmen and Don Jose, Aida and Ladames, and Papageno and Papagena joined my flock of chickens. As I learned more about chickens, as chickens became a part of our family life, including the fresh eggs on our breakfast table every morning, my vision of becoming an ostrich breeder started to take a different, more realistic shape. I couldn't say it aloud to anybody. The more serious your dream becomes, the more fragile it appears. If I'd say it aloud, it would evaporate, and the dream would never come true, I felt.

I frequented the science museum to see the chicken incubators. On weekdays, I would squat in front of them and watch the activities inside for hours without being disturbed. They let me in for free because I sometimes brought in fertilized eggs for the incubators. No matter how many times I saw the scene, the spectacle in the incubator overwhelmed me. The newly hatched chickens especially caught my attention. Their down still damp and bloody, exhausted from the tedious labor of coming out into the world, the baby chicks tottered along the glass walls, tweeting weakly. Due to their bloody appearance, they looked as if they were dying, instead of just having been born. And there were about two dozen other bloody chickens, reeling and staggering, or tweeting and pecking or lying and resting.

The resting ones were still. With their little batteries run out, they were flat on the floor, their short legs and little wings sprawled in every way, their tiny tongues sticking out, their eyelids half-closed showing the whites of their eyeballs, with clotted blood all over the bodies. *Gosh, they're actually dead*, I thought.

Almost a quarter of them seemed dead; I didn't know they had to risk their lives to come out into life.

But I found out, after a while, in five minutes or so, those dead chickens rose up like voodoo ghosts and started to waddle about to explore their little world as if nothing had happened. Meanwhile, those who had been toddling would pass away in a flash, like drunken hobos falling asleep in the gutters of graveled road.

This repetitive cycle of newborn chicks—tweet and toddle, drunk dead, up, toddle and tweet—never bored me. These gory creatures were full of life!

And they constantly reminded me of my father's father, Grandpa Tomizo, so-called Grandpa Tom, who died during my incubator years, when I was thirteen.

He showed his first sign of a drinking problem after he had moved into a hospital for nephritis complicated by gout, a half year before his death. Grandpa Tom had been drinking since he was twelve, but, mind you, always moderately. He had never caused trouble to others because of his love for liquor. If you could just listen, at his wake, how his friends and relatives praised the way Grandpa Tom used to drink!

They would lament his death as they filled each other's glass with Grandpa Tom's favorite vodka, calling his drinking style noble and humble at the same time.

He was always quiet, smiling occasionally, sitting in the corner with his glass of vodka and a piece of fresh chili pepper in his hands. He would nibble the pepper and slurp the liquor; slurp the vodka and nibble the pepper. Thus he would sit for hours. His relatives talked and laughed at his funeral about the way Grandpa Tom had been happy as a clam during Prohibition with his handmade little distillery in the basement, making his own liquor from sweet potatoes.

But at the end of his life, Grandpa Tom behaved like a wicked alcoholic just because he had never lived in a place as dry as the hospital, even during Prohibition.

He really didn't know what to do. The nurses treated him like an alcoholic, and this made us really sad. We pleaded with his nurses to let him have a drop of vodka and he would be contented, but they would just nod and smile with their eyes saying, *Sure. That's what you always say.* So finally one day, Grandpa Tom sneaked out of the hospital and toddled across the boulevard on his gouty feet to a liquor shop. He bought a mini-bottle of vodka, and restraining his excitement, he toddled back across the road to the hospital. He later told Ma it had taken him an hour to cross the street twice. He waddled up the stairs and climbed up on his bed. When he put his hand into his bosom to take out his mini-bottle, a nurse came into his room.

When we heard this story from another nurse, we all blushed in shame and exclaimed. "How dare you, tyrants! He's finishing his life! A drop will do him good, no harm!"

The nurse gave us a dirty look as if we were grumbling nonsense, so we decided on our way home, the next time we would come visit him, we would bring him some vodka in a coffee pot.

Grandpa Tom could not even finish a spoonful of vodka. Three drops were enough for him. He blushed like a bride and said thank you to us. After we talked a little about the weather, school and the nursery, he became drowsy so we left. He died two months later. We managed to smuggle in the coffee pot every other week in his last months. Every time we walked into the hospital with his coffee pot hidden in the bottom of Ma's tote bag, I glanced back at the street where Grandpa had crossed twice for his vodka, and then I think of chickens in the incubators. If Grandpa Taketora is a titanic hero in our family epic, Grandpa Tom is an old friendly gnome in our family fables.

After Grandpa Tom died, I stopped visiting the incubators. I was not only busy with my ever increasing chickens—now there were a dozen of them—but also I had started going out with this eighth grader, whose name I don't want to mention. Well, I didn't hate him or like him, but I went out with him only because that's what everybody was supposed to do and he wasn't as bad as the rest of the herd. School had turned into a strange place when I became a seventh grader—suddenly, all the girls started to flirt like crazy. They were blinking their eyes harder than ever. I could hear them tweeting *coquet, coquet, coquet.*

The boys appeared like half-grown chickens with their tiny cockscombs and their ill-proportioned, stretched bodies in mixed feathers. They were ugly and angry like my cockerels. I wished I'd had a garbage lid at school to protect myself from those half-chicken, half-rooster boys. That's what I used at home to shield myself from the cockerels.

Ma became frantic when she found out I had a date, not because she thought I shouldn't, but because my brother had none. She insisted that George must be secretly popular at school. I said no. Being such a short, ugly, clumsy, shy thing, how could he interest those half-chicken, half-coquette girls? Then Ma would accuse me of not introducing nice girlfriends of mine to him.

"Since you are the big sister, Eleanor," Ma went on, "you have to take care of your little brother for the rest of your life. It's your duty to introduce him to nice girls. They must like him."

The idea of taking care of my brother for the rest of my life depressed me.

Ma had her own theory. She insisted that George had no date because of his hearing problem. He had been hit by a Sunday school bus when he was six. I saw him tossed up like a volleyball on the bonnet. After he was carried away to the hospital by the same bus, the neighbor kids who had been watching the accident from the distance rushed to me, their faces all glowing in excitement. *Did he die? Did he die?* That's all they wanted to know. No, he didn't. He didn't even break his leg. But the shock to his head caused this hearing problem—he could not catch high-pitched tones very well, especially when the sound came from behind. So according to Ma, George must be missing the pretty chicks tweeting behind him at school every day; the chicks must be desperately curious about him.

I knew that was not the case, but I had no good counterargument, so I just let her believe in her theory. I had no time to check for chicks tweeting behind my brother. I was already busy with my chicks: Romeo wanted to monopolize all the hens, and poor Don Jose was always getting beaten up by Romeo. Carmen would flirt with Romeo openly. I had to put Romeo into a separate cage before jealous Don Jose stabbed Carmen with a dagger or innocent Juliet stabbed herself.

There were more sexual confusions. When I was sixteen, Papageno turned out to be a hen and Papagena a rooster. Again, I thought about complaining to Pedro the Mexican chick dealer. They were the last chickens I bought from the old poussin man. I actually went to see him. By then I knew where he lived. In his shack, I saw the same two willow baskets, one for girls and one for boys. Since Pedro couldn't always keep an eye on the chickens, some of them would jump out of the baskets. He grabbed them and put them back, but sometimes he couldn't tell from which basket the chicken had sneaked out. And poor Pedro had no way to tell whether the chicken was a boy or a girl. Only the chicken farmer could tell. The poussin man just bought chicks from him.

I returned home without telling him what had happened to Papageno and Papagena. Pedro kept telling me I have to study hard. *Listen to your parents. Listen to your teachers. Listen to your friend Pedro's advice. Learn to read. Don't skip school.*

I never did, but what made me sad more than anything else was that old Pedro could not tell roosters from hens, and that's the knowledge I craved most and I didn't know who else to look up to, except this wrinkled man with a Chinese pipe. On my way back, I became more determined about my future plan. Now I felt I was ready to tell my parents what I wanted to do. I had a lot more to learn about the creatures. I wanted to go to college to become a veterinarian. I thought it was a matter of course.

So I told Ma and Pa that I wanted to go to college to become a vet right after I reached home.

"What?" Pa grimaced at my confession.

Ma interrupted him, "I'm sorry, Eleanor. We don't have the money. I'm sorry. We can't even afford to go back to Japan. I mean, for the funeral. Grandpa Taketora died. We've just got a telegram."

It was a remote death. He was my mythic hero, but I didn't know his face, and I hadn't heard his voice. Somebody had died far away on the other side of the Earth.

Somebody I knew only in stories and in letters. He had a big wish for me. But the wish was very remote from my real life. Ma was crying. I tried to cry so as not to be rude to her and dead Grandpa. But tears just didn't come. I had to give up crying. My eyes got tired from too much squinting.

A week later, I had to face a closer death. Romeo died, having being bit by a weasel. I found him cold and stiff in the little corner behind Pa's greenhouse one morning.

Two weeks later, Tosca died. I suspect the December chill did it. My first chicken.

Chicken-One.

This time I didn't have to try to cry.

It was disturbingly easy.

We sort of avoided talking about Grandpa Taketora. I noticed my parents were exchanging letters with Ma's relatives. But it was too sad to think about him and not to be able to go to his funeral, or his burial, or even to see his grave. We all tried to concentrate on our business, chickens and college in my case. Then good news came. Some girl asked George to go out skating with her. My brother got a date! See, it's not because of his hearing problem! We just needed some patience.

Ma was ecstatic. She had known the day would come, but she couldn't believe her eyes when St. Valentine's Day came and my brother got cards from two girls he didn't even know. He was becoming popular. Now freed from the duty of introducing nice girls to my brother, which I never did actually, I could focus on my future. I had to manage to go to college all by myself. I had to put my chickens into one of Pa's chrysanthemum greenhouses so that they wouldn't freeze to death. I had to go out with my date. I had to study, especially biology.

It was one afternoon before the spring Equinox when a parcel arrived at our place. Pa had ordered the 1959 Directory of Japanese-Americans from the Daily Japanese-American Times in Los Angeles. It was as thick as Pa's hardcover Bible.

He had paid the publisher to have his nursery's name printed in bold letters. I had just come home from school and, munching on toast, I watched him thumb through the directory. After checking Suzuki Nursery in bold both in English and Japanese and browsing other names like Auntie Satoko and other Japanese friends, he went back to the greenhouse. I reached for the Persian blue book to see what it was like and got bored right away because there were so many Chinese characters I couldn't read. I discovered there were many Suzukis all over America, even in a city called Boring, Oregon, where only three Japanese families lived.

My eyes stopped at the advertisement section in the middle of the book. They were full of photographs: banks, many Mount Fujis, Tokyo Tower, airlines, rich farms in California, exotic places in Japan, girls in kimonos, etc. There was a full-page photograph of President Eisenhower, too, with the title *Supporter of World Peace* in Japanese. Then there was this photograph of diligent looking young Japanese men and women, all dressed in white lab coats, with smiles on their faces. A man in the center was joyfully examining something blurry in his hand under a lamp. He seemed to be examining something very curious. Two women were smiling and watching him courteously at his sides.

The caption screamed on the top: *A Secure Future in a High Paying Job! Earn $50 to $150 a Day!*

I was surprised at the amount of money, but I couldn't tell what sort of job the three people in the photograph were performing.

Smaller letters under the caption itemized the job's merits: *Job guaranteed upon graduation. Technicians are urgently needed. Servicing hatcheries in 42 states. Oldest & largest school. Write today for free catalogue.*

Under the photograph the advertisement read: *American Chick Sexing School, Long Beach, California.*

I studied the black and white photograph closer. It was hard to distinguish against the man's white lab coat, but he was surely holding a chicken upside down, checking the underside of the chicken's tiny wings. I could barely see its pointy beak and dotty eye in the blurred photograph. Under the lamp was a large wooden box divided into partitions, whose insides the photograph didn't show much, but now I could recognize a couple of little fluffy crowns peeking out of the box.

I flipped and fumbled through the book for more chick sexing schools. There were at least four other schools listed in the directory, including the one in our state of Washington. One of them put a small ad, explaining that determining a chicken's sex was very critical to evaluating its market value, but sexing newborn chickens required a trained, professional eye. Only a certified "chick sexist" could tell hens from roosters from their appearance. This chick sexing technique had been originally developed and systematized in Japan and the trained Japanese's discerning eyes and delicate hands were in great need in the chicken farming industry. The certified chick sexists were living proof of how Japanese Americans could contribute to tomorrow's American society, etc.

My head was throbbing. I regretted that I grew up in a suburban nursery, not in a city farm where I would have learned all about certified chick sexists. The scattered pieces of my future vision came to fit neatly together in my future perfect life. I could make my living by handling yellow fluffy chickens every day. I would save the money and would go to a veterinary college, or I could even go to college while sexing chickens every day. This was what I wanted in life! To become a vet, sexing chickens. I had to tell my parents. But I had to calm down first. I had to choose the best time and place to propose my wonderful plan.

That night, I dreamt myself sexing chickens in a chicken farm in the clouds. It had all the highlights of my life, my life with chickens. In the dream, I could somehow tell chickens' sex by gently holding each chicken in my palm. My palms sensed their sex intuitively through the sensation of the fluff's fidgeting in my hands. I grabbed the chickens one by one, exclaiming, *Chicken-One, Chicken-Two, Chicken-Three*, and

I could see at least a thousand chickens lining up to the edge of the cloud patiently waiting to have their sexes determined by me. This mere sight put me into total euphoria. Even the clouds were tinted sunny yellow with patches of creamy ivory. I was putting chickens into a pink willow basket or a blue one, exclaiming, "Chicken-One! Girl! Tosca! Chicken-Two! Boy! Tristan! Chicken-Three! Girl! Isolde! Chicken-Four! Boy! Romeo! Chicken-Five! Boy again! Papageno!" and on and on I went. Old Pedro was there, too, smiling, squatting and smoking his long pipe by the two baskets.

Behind him were ostriches curiously peeping into the baskets with their necks curved, wowing at my dexterity.

When I reached Chicken-Ninety, I felt a new, yet familiar kind of sensation in my hands. I couldn't tell its sex. Gradually opening my palms to uncage the chicken, I saw its beady eyes on the yellow ball of down. It had somewhat a longish face for a chicken and strands of longer, whiter feathers above its ebony eyes. Our eyes met.

"Hello," I said to the chicken, and the chicken replied, "We've finally met."

Right then, I opened my eyes.

I walked into the living room in my pajamas, still in a dream state. What a happy dream. I hadn't had such a nice dream for more than a year. My footsteps were light.

Maybe today is a good day to bring up my plan to Ma and Pa, I thought. The dream must be a good sign.

Passing through the living room to go to the kitchen for breakfast (*and notice, kitchen sounds similar to chicken!* I said to myself), I glanced at George, saying good morning, which I don't do very often nowadays. He was standing in front of the fireplace, yawning and stretching. He nodded at me, resting his right hand on his hip and looking outside through the lacy curtain. The pose looked familiar to me. I looked at him carefully again.

Oh my God, I said to myself, *Oh my God.* I stood gaping, trying to scream, but I was choked and all I could do was to let pitiable sirens of strange vowels out of my trembling throat.

George had accidentally posed the same way Grandpa Taketora does in his portrait hung above George's tousled head: the right hand on his hip, his face slightly averted. The two identical figures made me realize that they also had identical faces.

Lean noses, thick eyebrows, long faces—if you'd take off Grandpa's glasses, pluck off several sprouts of hair from George's chin, smooth out his dark pimples all over his face and neatly comb his thick black hair, they would look like the same man in the future and the past. Furthermore, I realized that the last chicken, the ninetieth chicken in my dream, had the same face as well in a chicken sort of way. Now I knew why George had suddenly got dates after Grandpa's death. Looking back, I thought George's face had started to change slightly about three months ago, the time Grandpa had died.

Before that, George hadn't looked like Grandpa Taketora at all.

"Oh no," I said to myself, this time aloud, "Oh no. Grandpa's summoning us from the netherworld. We are dead!"

"What are you talking about?" George cried.

Our parents came into the living room from the kitchen.

"Enough, kids," Pa said.

"My, Eleanor!" Ma ran up to me. "What's wrong? You're so pale!"

I told them George looked like Grandpa. They looked at the portrait, George, and back at the portrait again. They seemed amazed at this discovery but didn't understand what I meant. They took it as something wonderful: George was becoming a mature man.

I had to add, still choking, "And I saw Grandpa Taketora in my dream this morning."

They fell silent.

"You know what," Ma opened her mouth after a while, "It's been ninety days since Grandpa died."

This fact chilled me even more, but she was smiling at me, sorrowfully, but smiling.

I couldn't tell them about the details of my chick sexing dream. I couldn't tell them he was Chicken-Ninety. How could I? They must be imagining Grandpa Taketora in his shroud, standing on the cloud, beckoning the two of us to heaven.

"He's calling you two," Ma continued. "You've never met Grandpa, and he couldn't see you two, either. He must have longed to see your faces, don't you think?"

Grandpa Taketora always counted the days left before I turned sixteen. Every letter was a countdown. He could wait only until he could see his great-grandchild.

But he hadn't met me, either. He had to see me and George first, before he saw his hypothetical great grandchild. We were his first grandchildren.

Pa put his hands on our shoulders and said, "Do you want to visit Japan? Do you want to say hello to your grandfather in Omura?"

So we went to Japan, me and George.

My parents could afford tickets only for the two of us. We took a boat. Everything went like a dream. The Earth was curved in a smaller scale in Japan. Mountains, rivers, fields, houses—everything was steep and tiny. We were in a miniature country. My mother's cousins and siblings were gentle, but neither of us understood their dialect. We were clumsy, not knowing how to sit on the floor, to take off our shoes, or to use the toilet. Our Japanese was awkward. They watched us behave like aliens with curious and persistent smiles.

Grandpa's house smelled salty and smoky. We saw his leather chair above which his portrait had been hung before it came to our house. We didn't say anything about the portrait. I found many things surprisingly familiar and dear, but also many other things remote. Probably everyone finds any foreign land this way: familiar and odd.

The day we visited Grandpa's grave on the hill that commands Omura Bay, cherry trees were blossoming. Many folds of hills surrounding the bay had started to blush in pale pink. The bay where Grandpa swam across as a twelve-year-old was much smaller than the titanic bay I had pictured when I had heard the epic. We heard the engines of fishing boats coming home. I couldn't see the boats because of the diffused reflections on the water. I could only hear the sound.

number 2 pencils for the white cat

Mr. Crow is a corporate accountant, but, to tell the truth, he is a closet novelist. Whenever Mr. Crow runs out of ideas to write about, he switches his polished ebony fountain pen to a number 2 school pencil to return to the basics, to feel the friction that every word creates on the paper.

Mr. Crow lines up new number 2 school pencils on his writing desk, and, ritualistically, he sharpens each pencil with his pocket knife, at his desk by the window.

Wooden shavings fall into the dust bin he holds between his knees. He concentrates on the sound that the knife and the wood make. He inhales the friction heat and the mixed odor of ebony and clay that rises from the tip of the pencil.

Every time Mr. Crow sharpens his number 2 school pencils, every time he has writer's block, a white cat comes to the window, attracted by the calm, regular rhythm of the pencil sharpening. Then it sits by the window and stares at Mr. Crow's hands steadily sharpening the number 2 school pencils. The white cat is mesmerized by the movements of Mr. Crow's hands, the way the pencil is tilted, how the wooden shavings shed off the pencil like dead leaves. The white cat gets a little cross-eyed, absorbed by Mr. Crow's pencils.

One night, when Mr. Crow is sharpening his pencils, not knowing what to write, the white cat comes to his window as usual. This time, the cat is so mesmerized by Mr. Crow's pencil sharpening, that it meows in an ecstatic yet creepy voice, as it rolls itself upside down, lying on its back. Mr. Crow opens the window for the first time. The white cat presses its cheek hard against the pencil in Mr. Crow's hand, sniffs the ebony and clay, licks the tip, and starts to bite and eat the pencil.

Half an hour later, the white cat finishes all the number 2 school pencils on Mr. Crow's desk. It looks up at Mr. Crow and burps three times and starts to tell him the following story:

Here I omit the story for editorial reasons.

The dawn comes and the cat finishes its story. Of course, Mr. Crow writes it down frantically. He publishes it. It becomes a national bestseller. It is translated into thirty-six languages. Since Mr. Crow has no writer's block any more, he doesn't sharpen pencils. He writes with his new Mont Blanc. He has a dozen Mont Blancs. Since he doesn't sharpen number 2 pencils any more, the white cat doesn't visit his study window anymore.

Five years go by.

Now Mr. Crow has published ten more novels. He has moved into a mansion in Switzerland. He lives there all by himself.

One full-moon night in October, the white cat visits Mr. Crow's studio window, though he is not sharpening his pencils any more. The cat stares hard at Mr. Crow through the window pane.

Mr. Crow senses right away that the white cat wants to be repaid for his success. It is going to claim, he is afraid, his first-born child. But he doesn't have any children since he doesn't have a wife or mistresses. So Mr. Crow tells the white cat in his gentlest way possible that he cannot offer the cat his first-born child. The cat stares at him without a word and walks away.

Since that night, the white cat has started to invite itself to Mr. Crow's window.

"What do you want?" Mr. Crow asks, "My soul? My money? Tell me!"

But the cat says nothing. Its face shows no expression. It stares at him and goes away.

Two years later, Mr. Crow finds the white cat dead under the fallen maple leaves in his backyard. He realizes then what the white cat wanted was more pencils.

More number 2 pencils for the white cat.

the source of my blue

THE BLUE—ITS SHADES IN SEVEN VEILS, PEACOCK, pearl, Prussian, cerulean, gentian, violaceous, morning glorious—heavenly blue to take a trip, sky blue, holly blue, and Adonis blue, these are volatile cobalt lepidoptera from inside abalones, flapping out of ear shells, quivering on a shy viola, hydrangea in early summer, gentian in autumn, bellflower, columbine in the evening... and seven more layers upon robin's egg, baby and duck, powder and Alice blue. They merge into the dull Nile, flowing down the canvas under the mist of spattered sapphire, under the mackerel sky. This view is from the bottom of the ocean, the atmospheric world imagined by a monkfish, a world seen through a thousand leaves of guanine foils and fish scales floating in the undulating aquamarine, the heaving ultramarine and the ripples of azure, the liquid lapis lazuli, precious stones from beyond the sea. At the bottom, a dark aniline blue vaguely traces voluptuous human curves—

perhaps a slack of upper arm, or a swell of abdomen. It is a solid curved surface in precipitated blue.

"I knew the painter," I finally gasp to my friend, still absorbed in the blues. This enormous painting occupies half of the wall in front of us.

"Are you okay?" my friend asks. "You look pale."

"I didn't know he still painted," I smile at myself. "I remember he quit, saying painting was not a serious business."

I sense my friend has gone to another room where her and my pieces are exhibited—honorable mentions—but cannot help uttering, "Why did he?"

The last time I saw him, he was on the platform waiting for a train—he was in uniform, we were both in school uniforms. He declared he'd quit painting, being ambitious in the most conventional way—wanted to become a lawyer or something—thought painting would hinder him from advancing his career. Stupid man. Art had no obligation in his life. For him, inspiration was an everlasting spring you could abandon at will. But is it really him—the painter? Such hues of infinitely mute colors.... No more audacious contrasts, decisive contours. No trace of brutal strokes with harsh, flat brushes. I feel a human presence next to me and I assume it is my friend. I turn to her, ready to speak, and it is *him*, not my friend, who has materialized.

"I'd been standing behind you for a while." His voice sounds lower than I remembered. "So how are you?" He clutches my hand and elbow, his grip so tight that the bases of our thumbs lock. "I just saw your piece; I could name it right away," he says, still shaking my hand.

"Yeah, I never grow up." I feel ashamed when I hear myself sounding bashful. "Congratulations to *you*. What a surprise. I didn't know you still painted."

He stares into my eyes, tilting his head and gathering his brows, without a word for a few seconds, his black pupils always indifferent. He opens his mouth, closes it, and then opens it again, like a goldfish, now groaning, "You know what."

"What?" I begin to feel I once knew this person.

"Nah, forget it." He waves me away and faces his painting. "It shouldn't be here, to tell you the truth. It doesn't want to be here." His eyes turn narrow at the bluish wall; I look at the two as a tableau: a painter and his painting. Is the painting part of him, or a being separate from him? The person I knew never seemed to brood in such blues.

We are standing at the platform waiting for a train. We have left the municipal museum. Outside is still chilly, but it is a sunny afternoon and the platform is facing west. I've let my rapid intercity train go since he insisted on taking a local one. He lives in a smaller town on my way home.

The local train has taken in highschoolers at the previous stop. It is mildly crowded. Girls in navy skirts dazzle me. They look dauntless. We stand hanging on to straps, and our conversation begins with predictable threads: our mutual acquaintances and our updates—his medical schooling and my apprenticeship at a graphic design studio—while the train passes the bowling alley we all frequented and the soda parlor where its constantly depressed owner took half an hour to prepare six glasses of soda.

Three highschool girls are giggling and nudging each other and giggling some more. Their quick yet obvious glances are cast at a handsome boy in school black, sitting neatly in the corner, with his fat leather satchel on his lap. He appears to be concentrating on looking self-contained.

"You know what," he says for the second time with his impersonal stare.

"What?" This time I feel slightly impatient.

"I had this feeling," so he begins, "a feeling I never experienced before, something I can't name, but I felt I might have known it before I'd had it. A sad sentiment, a sort of resignation, yet full of expectations, lukewarm despair, a sentiment of presentment, without resentment, a sense of dead end, but beautiful. Something amazingly beautiful. That feeling came to me, and I knew it would leave me soon, so I absolutely had to grasp it.

"But how? That is always the question.

"I try music. I take over my sister's piano and *bing*, strike a key, *bing*, another key, and one after another—faster, faster—and listen, here's a melody for my melancholy. But the music evaporates. It doesn't stay with my sentiment.

"I think of poetry. I know I'm fairly good at choosing words. I write one down, strike it out, write another, and strike it out again. I just don't get a strike, never slap-bang in the middle, no bull's eye, it's fairly accurate, a good approximation of.... *of what?* Now I'm determined to pursue it, but no matter what, you know, words are not *it*. Words are words. I feel defeated and give up on words.

"It has to be something direct—somehow I have to reach the core of it, its essence, the thing somewhere inside me. Yes, my guts, my dear. So I swallow an endoscope.

"The tube descends into the dark of my stomach. A solitary cave expedition deep under the ground to meet my troglodytic double. I guzzle the tube; the belly camera takes a photo. I blow it up. And here's my guts, reproduced with complete fidelity, a sedimentary gray stomach in my inner dusk."

He poses and cracks a wild smile at me, his eyes wide open. My lips part, but I swallow the intended words. They remain in *my* guts. I stare at my toes and say, "And that's your blue painting?"

"Not really," he admits. "You see, *I* was happy with it; that was the closest to the thing itself. But for others, it's rather incomprehensible, because, you see, after all, that thing is strange to others.

"It's too nude. It needs some cover-ups.

"As I added each layer of blue paint to the blown-up photograph, my guts withdrew from me, but all the while, I felt the rest of the world coming closer to it. Yes, by the end of it, it wasn't a duplicate of my guts, it was something else, somewhat like a separate being. But you still recognize my gastric lines in the background, don't you?"

I nod, disgusted, thinking of the opaque blue curves.

"And one day, my sister stole the painting. She's brought it to that competition. It's like having a twin brother—you sense what he feels from afar. It doesn't want to stay there, but I can't rescue my poor kidnapped organ. All I can do is think about it—you see, once it's ripped out of my guts, I must take care of it, talk to it, put it in the sun, take it for a walk, sing to it, water it, cover it up, write to it, but most of all, think of it." Here he quits his words.

I'm tempted to tell him to take a good care of his endoscoped guts, but I resist. He doesn't need my advice. I know he will look after it, will think of it, and will die happily alone with his blue viscera.

The train's doors open. He gets off, stepping back, once again squeezing my hand. He does not say goodbye. He says, "That's all," and leaves. I feel like I am watching a stranger on the platform. He is striding away, his gaze slightly up at the pale blue of the March sky.

milk bath

I

Now Miyuri has to spend four hours bathing all by herself. There is nothing to do in Minomachi but bathing. Six public hot-spring baths located along the two parallel Main Streets, which take you less than twenty minutes to walk through, are all Minomachi has to offer to tourists.

It is the middle of September—too early for the Japan Sea crabs which, in winter, city dwellers in Osaka and Kobe slobber over. It is too late for swimming. It is Saturday, and it is three o'clock in the afternoon—too early to get poached in the hot spring though Miyuri has been jolted for five hours in the train from Osaka for this purpose. This is not exactly what she intended, however. She has a question to ask him: something she's been holding back.

Though her boyfriend cannot join her in the same bath, two of them going to the baths together would make a great difference: finishing the bath at the arranged time and sharing a bottle of soda with him on the ripped faux-leather sofa in the front lobby, describing to each other the designs of the bathroom and the dressing room, competing in weight (the lighter the winner, of course), browsing cheap souvenir shops, rambling through shabby alleys. Those trifling pleasures are a serious matter in a hot spring resort. But he needed an undisturbed sleep.

Her boyfriend, an obscure cartoon artist, owed her a holiday and worked day and night to meet a deadline that had long past. He had fretted in the train all the way to Minomachi. Last night, the steamed cod milt served at the inn turned out to be too rich for him, and fever knocked out the poor wasted fellow. He was too frazzled to sleep through the night. This morning, he seemed more exhausted than the night before and begged her to be left alone so that he could get some sleep. She promised to meet him at seven at their room in the guesthouse.

Miyuri goes out of the inn, takes a bus and a boat across the river to a basaltic cavern and to a tiny aquarium—where the crisp smoke of grilled fish from the well-ventilated cafeteria puts the visitors in front of the tanks into an ichthyo-logical/phagous dilemma while they are trying to impress their children (or girlfriends) with the story of salmon that travel thousands of miles to their home river.

She returns to the front door of the inn, then glances at her watch. Three o'clock. She has exhausted all the sights already. The last thing she can do is to indulge in the six public baths from the first dip to the last drop for four hours until the Sleeping Beauty wakes up. Dressed in the guesthouse yukata, toting the hotel's small wicker basket that contains a plastic soap case and a face towel, slipping on clogs (the hotel name is also printed, of course), she flows out to Main Street, seen off by the landlady, and stands for a moment in the quiet, bright street, embarrassed at being the only one wearing a bathrobe on the street.

II

The narrow town of Minomachi, like a dragon or rather a baby snake lying at the bottom of a ravine, is more of a gloomy mountain village than a seaside resort. On both sides of the trickling river are willow and cherry lined streets, barely wide enough for a bus to pass. The old-fashioned but newly built stone bridges connect both streets, along which stand haughty hotels of wooden houses easily a hundred years old. Every gate is magnificent. A shrunken doorman in a happi coat is loitering at a deserted carriage entrance in the front yard, scratching the graveled ground with his sandaled toe and chewing the edge of the towel around his neck. Inside the vestibules await exquisite courtyards—landscaped with, for example, stone lampposts and cultivated mosses—that whet her curiosity (Miyuri the courtyard aficionado) but their overwhelming opulence and off-seasonal emptiness discourage her from peeking inside.

Between these luxurious hotels, thrifty inns, crammed like sunburnt paperbacks squeezed between gold embossed encyclopedias, expose their crumbling eaves and jerrybuilt lumber spines. They do not have any extra estate to waste for gardens. Their buildings have more than three stories, and their bay windows face the street. Relaxed in his yukata, an old man is looking down the street from the second floor of an paperback hotel, leaning against the latticework. His cigarette ashes snow down on Miyuri's shoulder. From the street, she can look up and see most of his suite's ceilings. She knows that the suite holds nothing of interest to her, or for any Japanese tourist for that matter—a typical hot spring ryokan furnishing: a hardwood floored narrow drawing room with a bay window and a six to eight tatami-matted room with a tea table. This kind of room has no secret: everyone knows what he will find inside before checking in.

The inn that Miyuri has reserved is, in consideration of their budget, one of those paperback guesthouses, antiquated and compact. The meager landlady in a blue dress ushered the two up into a room in the rear of the house on the second floor: a dim, six tatami-matted nook with a window facing the lichened wall of the valley a few feet away. Entering the room, she smelled the aged, full-bodied bouquet of the mold and the brewing moisture. But it was too late to retreat.

This town is a fine miniature of the ideal medicinal hot spring resort. The whole town is devoted to realize its balneal fantasy. Strip bars in a dim side alley (A bent woman beckons from an obscure corner), pinball machines and rifle games (Packages of cheap chocolate and musky cigarettes on the revolving round shelves. Cork bullets. Smack! Smack!). All forms of entertainment are waiting for you behind the aluminum sliding doors under the gimcrack signs. The small liquor shops prosper selling the local sake. Every souvenir shop displays the identical items for the same price: large rice crackers, smoked cuttlefish, dried horse mackerel, key chains, flashy-colored picture cards, stuffed animals.... All the details compose parts of a replica—a replica of a long lost Japanese hot spring village.

Descending the lane into the depth of the gorge, Miyuri imagines how intangible she would look from the panorama tower at the ropeway station on the summit, where Miyuri and her boyfriend climbed yesterday. The tower is above the tip of the slender serpent tail. It commands the snaky figure of the town in a full bird's-eye view. Those tourists in the valley, don't they look like spermatozoa penetrating into the cavern, crawling here and there along the stream? She fancies another couple on the view roof, who may at this moment be gazing down at her tottering along the street.

The hot spring town and the trickling brooklet are stuck in the mountains' cleavage—moderate rain would cause the rivulet to swell to a surge, which would flow into the main stream behind the railway station in the bottomland, no higher than sea level. The main stream does not meander and the water is still. The dry riverbed would become sopping wet when the tide is full.

The reedy marshes across the river hold a great heronry. Under the flush of a mackerel evening sky, thousands of egrets tinted in coral would shower in unison, flapping down to the sough. Beyond the heronry, if it were cloudy as yesterday, the seagreen and the mintgreen of the morass grass, the moonstone blue of the river surface absorbing the muted light, the celadon blue of the Japan Sea laced with the breaker waves in oxidized silver, and the liquid jade green sky with fat cream poured in—all those colors would be fused and mirror on one's cornea behind the cool moist veil of the early autumn. The horizon must be the end of this world, the world of the living, but one would not see the line. One would only smell the soothing mist that blurs the border between the two worlds.

III

Turning the gentle curve, Miyuri comes out near the approach of a massive stone bridge where willows rustle. Between the willows, she finds *Yanagi-yu*, the Willow Bath. The stone monument at the entrance of this bathhouse reads that there had been no willow here until a certain novelist planted willows in front of this spa in his novella to romanticize its landscape. His last visit here was a week before he committed a double suicide with someone else's wife. Miyuri read his last note to his elder brother, in which the novelist described how he and his companion to the netherworld were making love at this moment and how happily they were going to die together. Double suicide was in fashion those days. A humanist writer, a pornographic suicide note. Post-coital bodies in the lukewarm water. Rustles of the willows brushing against the lovers' slackened bellies. Did he write it before undressing his love, or after they reached the climax and together went through a little death? The only authentic love suicide note is the one written while making love, whether alone or together. Did she read what he wrote? Did she reach where he reached, too? You come and die or you fail to come, try again, fail, and die. A phone always rings before a climax and your bladder becomes heavy, you press your abdomen hard, a doorbell rings, you want to cry, but your lachrymal glands are dry, this moment you are supposed to be making love, but all you can think of is your sore clitoris and that's when you decide you kill yourself for love. Now for the first time, she stands at the very place she has visited many times in his book.

The Willow Bath is a square bathplace—every part of the building is a golden-balanced rectangle. Miyuri likes the rustic bathroom inside. The whole floor, walls, and bathtub are made of maroon granite, whose surfaces have gained a smooth luster absorbing the permeating essence of the spring. It's a sunken bath like Roman or Chinese baths, that way the floor seems more spacious. The plain walls and the high ceiling hold a functional grace.

Miyuri gradually enters the water from the steps in the pool. The water is light and tepid. The hot spring in Minomachi does not remind her of the hot springs she's been familiar with. This is thoroughly transparent and odorless. The only feature is a strong salty taste, the common characteristic of any seaside hot spring. The hot spring in Miyuri's mind has the peculiar eggshell-burning odor of sulfur, the geothermal heat that you feel through the pavement, the chamois smoke belching and surging over the slate blue roofs, the rusty hotel balconies eaten by the sulfur steam, the muddy water in tattletale gray like weak cement, the bronze turbid water heavier than pure water, the colloid that does not plash when you walk inside, and your skin turns slick and smooth in the water. Some springs are toxic, so people just come and watch them. Some baths are too hot, so they steam rice and chicken or boil eggs until the water turns mild enough to bathe in. One spa does not spring hot water but heats the beach, where people are buried in a row with their heads sticking out like matchsticks. Miyuri was born and raised in volcanic Kyushu, and she has bathed in various hot springs. She has found that every hot spring is alive and has its character. But she finds the water in Minomachi lifeless. It lacks vigor, the vital power of spa, or say, the thermal energy of magma. Minomachi is a long, long gentle slope that never reaches the peak. Where the lovers never reach.

Miyuri is soaked in the warm water up to her neck, with her eyes closed and her lips apart, breathing slowly. The blood rushes up to her head, so she seats herself (her yet cool soft buttocks) on the edge of the pool to chill out. She hears a couple of aged male voices echoing over the partition wall. There are two old women in the woman's bath. They are washing themselves facing the faucets on the wall. As they have their own large bottles of shampoo, they must be local inhabitants. Tourists do not shampoo at public bath.

Miyuri gets into the water again. Then another old woman and seemingly her middle-aged daughter enter followed by three women in their mid-fifties, and the bathroom suddenly becomes busy, so Miyuri flees from the bath.

The floor of the dressing room is covered with a mat made of thinly torn bamboo, in taupe, tarnished from the straw ocher over time. The surface of the carpet is slippery because of the human grease and pressure over years. Miyuri notices, drying herself on the hotel towel, that her fingertips are not sodden. It is a matter of the osmotic pressure: because the concentration of salt in the spring water is greater than her body fluid, it does not provide moisture to her like normal baths, but it deprives her of water. Then Miyuri thinks, like any young woman would, that the bloat should subside and her body should get slimmer, and she becomes a little elated. She glances at the large mirror by the scale. She tells herself that she is not fat, but the truth is that gravity is gradually defeating her muscles. She soon sniffs away her fancy and smells her fingertips. She misses the pale maze relief on her fingertips that resembles the wrinkles on the cerebral cortex. The sodden relief has been always the token of the pleasure of bathing for her, but the water in Minomachi is too feeble to impress the mark on her body.

Hold me tight, my love, the woman says, but his grip is so tender. He has taken his pills already. The woman is left with her bottle to gobble. She has no choice, for he failed to leave his mark on her. She should leave at this moment.

IV

Outside it is fairly dark already though the wall clock in the lobby tells it's ten after four. The street lamps have not been lit yet. For myopic Miyuri, the world is dimmest at this time of the day. She has three more hours to bathe.

There are not many people on the street, but chartered buses frequently pass by. Being off the season, but still a weekend, many overnight tourists from big cities may come. Miyuri has to step aside when the buses pass by. Then a red minicar with a young family and a spoiled college student's shiny SUV follow.

She deviates from the street and strays into an alley to avoid the cars. There they still come roaring by. It is worse on the narrow road. The exhaust fumes adhere to her washed skin. The noise of engines that she's never heard so close terrifies her. They are everywhere on the Earth. You hail in the Gobi Desert and a cab will stop in a second; cans and plastic bags drift to deserted shores. A smoky dullness like lees slowly sinks to the bottom of her stomach. Before anger flames up, she hears the pattering of rain that dampens down her indignation.

She checks the map pursed in her yukata sleeve as she hurries to the nearest bathhouse, *Jizo-yu*, the Ksitigarbha Bath, which turns out to be closed that day. The heavy raindrops spatter *poco a poco* and print a black polka-dot pattern on the pavement. They reach her scalp and start dripping down her nose.

V

Fortunately, another bath is not far from the Ksitigarbha Bath. In *Gosho-yu*, the Palace Bath, some princess bathed eight hundred years ago. The front monument quotes words from a novel by another dead writer (this novelist did not commit suicide—he had visited Minomachi to heal his wounds from a street-car accident), in which the Palace Bath is described "as deep as to reach his nipples." She enters the door with great expectation, for she has never bathed in such a deep bath before, but she will soon be disappointed. The novel was first published seventy years ago. The bath was rebuilt, of course, made hipbone deep in the age of liability.

A shriveled woman comes to greet her. She does not see any other person in the front lobby. Miyuri stoops down over her clogs to put them aside, but the lady hurries to her, saying, "No, no, no... I shall do it. Please, please come in."

There is a tiny courtyard, as small as a linen closet, beyond the glassed wall of the lobby. Under a dwarf stone lamp, now the misty rain is wetting the milky quartz beads covering the ground and the subtle shrubbery sticking out from underneath. The woman's bath inside has a more formal courtyard, composed of several ash and bamboo trees, a bamboo-woven screen, the dragon barbel grass as the underbrush, and a delicate stone lamp with an electric bulb in it.

She is the only person in the room.

Miyuri is fond of every courtyard in the world—Japanese, Chinese, and Spanish…. She does not care about the shallow bathtub anymore. Soaked in the lukewarm water in the favabean-shaped pool, looking at the foggy glitter upon the washed grass through the window, she is happy. There is a little fountain inside the pool. The fresh air flowing down from the ceiling windows keeps her head cool, while her body relaxes in the lush, thermal spring. The body is light in the salt water. She watches her belly dancing under the concentric ripples from the fountain. She kicks the wall of the bathtub and stretches herself, floating in the water, then swashes the water, dog paddling across the pool, and gets out to try the steam bath behind the glass door.

The salty steam flows out of the heavy door. She slowly steps in. A bluish marble bench in the long and narrow room faces the big window. Miyuri rubs the glass so she can see the garden through it.

Three nozzles on the ceiling swoosh the spa spring in fine mist. It whooshes, mizzles and swooshes, sprinkling minerals to refresh her organs. Miyuri lies supine on the marmoreal bench and closes her eyes, loosening up her muscles and draining all the energy out of her body. The myriad mist flocks on her eyelashes, grows into drops, rushing down her blushed cheeks. Cells separate and float, absorbing the ocean water. She takes a deep breath.

She hears the sound of the sliding door open and the murmur of voices. She raises her body and sits upright on the bench before six women come into the steam bath.

"Seven fat hips squeezed altogether on one bench!" says one of them aloud, and they all laugh together. Miyuri feels the hip of the woman next to her, cooler than hers, fresh and plump like hors d'oeuvre ham. Their rich bodies are signs of felicity. They transmit bliss to the people next to them. That is how they make one another happy. Miyuri tells herself that she should leave this crowded bench, but a delightful satisfaction makes her hesitate. The wives have Tokyo accents: their deep and bitter vowels are unique to Tokyo natives. People in the West never speak like that. Their chattering pleases Miyuri's ears like an exotic song. While Miyuri seeks the opportunity to leave, one of them stands up to get out, and so she follows the woman out of the steam bath.

In the main chamber of the bath, there are several women bathing and washing. Miyuri sits under the ceiling window to cool down. A middle-aged woman says hello and slides close to Miyuri.

"Where do you come from?"

The woman's voice is low and calm.

"I come from Kyoto. And you, Madame?"

"Yokohama. We've just been to Kyoto on our way here. I love Kyoto."

Yes, she knows every Japanese woman loves Kyoto, or, to be more precise, every woman knows every other woman loves Kyoto. Inside, Miyuri sneers at their idea of romantic Kyoto. Kyoto is a cursed city, Miyuri thinks. That is where all the memories have accumulated for centuries, and memories are never sweet, they are sour at best—usually bitter, often rotten. Once you live there a day longer than the tourists, you feel the damnation. Otherwise she wouldn't have escaped the city for a shabby spa resort. It's a kind of elopement, isn't it? Into a village created by double suicidal artists from a city created by paranoiacs.

Miyuri wonders if she has been an inhabitant of the Kyoto imagined by these women—rivers and mountains, stone steps and wooden bridges, (underneath, homeless men with their pet cats) geisha and maiko (and maiko-costumed tourists), noh and kabuki, combs and rouge, green tea and sweets, souvenir shops and townhouse cafés, cherry blossoms, fireflies (and students' fireworks and a police squad), maple trees, palaces and treasures, shrines and temples, pagodas. Tombs. Ruins. How can we feel nostalgic for something we have never lost nor possessed to begin with? Miyuri may be living in Kyoto as an index of the times past. Just thumb through to Section M.

The woman says that they visited Misora Hibari Memorial Museum in Kyoto. Lady Misora is a dead diva, the greatest star of their generation. Her parents watched Lady Misora sing on TV, and Miyuri wished for more fun shows, cartoons, perhaps. Whenever she saw her on TV, Lady Misora was shedding tears while singing. Her songs vaguely warned Miyuri against the universally depressing adult life. Now Miyuri likes Lady Misora's songs better—quietly dramatic and bitterly merry—as if that was one way to enjoy the misery of adult life.

After an hour she dries her body and comes out to the front lobby. The woman in the front recognizes her, and presents her with the right clogs from her guesthouse. The woman identifies the tourists by their clogs, matching the name of the hotel printed on their yukata with that on the clogs. Miyuri wants to show the Palace Bath's courtyards to her boyfriend, wants to share the view from the lobby, and wants him to reconnoiter the courtyard of the men's bath. She actually thinks of him for the first time in this long languid afternoon. So, she is fine by herself after all.

Miyuri has thought of herself as an independent woman, yet she's felt he would not live without her. Yes, she's self-centered, indulgent, she knows. But she's been wanting to ask him if—maybe, those suicidal writers had no chance to take baths by themselves for four hours, just be in the water, stroll and gaze at the sky, at a loss for what to do in the next few hours, few days… and the rest of their lives. This laziness, this loneliness might have spared them the final action. Then how fortunate she is to be left alone. How deliriously intoxicating and how simply terrible it is to be at someone's side forever.

VI

It has stopped raining outside. The street has become crowded with tourists, mostly middle-aged women in yukata. Those chartered buses must have poured out the tourists into the streets while she was in the Palace Bath. The closer she walks up to the mountain, the loftier the hotel buildings become, and the more people are wandering about in identical hotel-made yukatas. The sun has set—the river is lined with new retro gas lamps. Miyuri approaches *Kohnoyu*, the Crane's Bath, the largest bathhouse in Minomachi. It is five thirty, the peak of the evening bathing hour before dinner. The workers are running around the front door holding two pairs of clogs in each hand. Miyuri's brain feels steamed from the long bathing. She automatically enters the dressing room.

Tourists' chatter and the clatter of wooden pails fill the steamy air up to the high ceiling. The bath water is too deep and hot for her already poached body. Then she remembers that the landlady recommended the open-air bath in the Crane's Bath. She sees it through the glass wall—a bower on the stone-paved ground. She walks straight up to the door.

VII

Under the roof, rough rocks form a wild pool. At the back of the bower, the musk mallow, retaining its deep color of the summer, covers the ground. A short lamppost of malachite is among the mallow grass. Seven women are bathing in three groups. Miyuri sits alone in the lukewarm liquid and observes them. The discussion by three women of nineteen or twenty years old on the varieties of pubic hair growth amuses her. All seven women are either thin or heavy—no moderation. One woman is marvelously fat. She fascinates Miyuri. She reminds her of her favorite nude photograph, a Japanese souvenir for Victorian gentlemen to enjoy with special spectacles. A woman is combing her hair after a bath, with her breasts bared out of her shabby cotton kimono. She pulls her long, abundant hair horizontally across her face. Her face is hidden behind the hair, which must be the photographer's artifice. The focus of the picture is the lushness of her brachia and breasts. Her upper arms are well muscled, but they are not built like a Hellenic Venus with impressive biceps. A considerable amount of fat muffles around her muscle. Her arms look like tanned, shining cylinders and both her breasts form perfect hemispheres. Every curved surface of her skin is stuffed with fat and muscle. Nothing slackens. Her stocky body almost threatens Miyuri. One does not find such an arrogant, haughty beauty overflowing with vivacity in this country any more, and probably never will again.

In the past, Minomachi was a balneotherapeutic place, not a sightseeing spot. People visited the town to cure their wounds. A woman would massage her limbs. A lacerated scar on a woman's shoulder blade would turn to mauve in the warm water. A maimed malleolus would be soaked in the serum hot spring. A large macula in an animal shape—maybe a mouse—under a woman's right bosom. Mammocks of glass emerging from the margaric skin. A woman complaining about her migraine. A young mother mundifying her baby's wound mumbling a mantric prayer. Heal us, mellifluous water. Warm us to the marrow. Mosses in motley colors on the rocks. Musty mushrooms would emerge among the mosses. Leaf mold mulching the feet of maple trees. The moon in the murky sky would mirror on the mellow water.

Their breasts would not be distorted by the wired brassieres. Their stocky waists would not be buckled up to the last inch. Their fingernails would not be enameled in red. Their thick black hair would be neither permanently waved nor bleached. Women are beautiful today. How perfect they look! Yet how shadowy they are. The still-life spring of Minomachi won't do to put the once dismembered body parts back together. Mothers suckling their babies on the streetcars have been replaced by the bikini girls in advertisement photos on the commuter trains. All we have is this imaginary memory of milk bath.

Two summers ago in Bali, Miyuri visited a small art museum, exhibiting the paintings by a German artist who had settled and died in Bali in the first half of the nineteenth century. A German Gauguin, so to speak. He had married a Balinese woman and had painted women in the island, who all had worn nothing but their traditional sarongs. They were working, dancing and resting spontaneously in his paintings. The Balinese now, even men, wore shirts to hide their chests from the eyes of each other and the outsiders. An old European woman sighed an audible sigh and said to her partner in English, "I'm sorry Balinese today has lost their innocence."

Innocence? This is not your shelter from the tumult of civilization. Miyuri was sorry that *that* woman had not yet lost her innocence. Would that ever happen? An irresponsible anger surged in Miyuri, but dullness and shame soon suffocated that anger.

That morning, Miyuri had talked with the hotel manager. He had been impressed by the economic prosperity in Japan, like every average Balinese had.

"I hope more Japanese companies will come to Bali. They work hard. I think we should develop our land more," he said.

"Why, I wouldn't like Bali to become busy and ugly. Your land has a priceless charm. You shouldn't destroy it. You'll regret it some day."

The manager smiled serenely and said, "I don't think so."

Miyuri did not understand. On the other hand she knew well the charm could be worthless to them indeed.

The Paradise is lost a priori. The beauty is never to be regained. It only exists in the souvenir photographs neatly boxed up with a pair of spectacles, forgotten in the dim smoking room. Only the memory remains. A fake memory, the banal balneal fantasy, but the only legitimate memory, desperately needed. Miyuri needs it, the hotel manager needs it, the couple at the museum need it, people in Minomachi need it. The villagers make painstaking efforts to copy the Minomachi in novels just to disappoint us. But we cannot stop making those clumsy efforts.

The two lovers cannot die at the exact same moment. The other always comes late, or not at all.

VIII

The musty odor is mingled with the smell of her boyfriend's sweat in the guesthouse's room. His steady breathing makes sounds like a steam engine slowing down. It is a sign that he is fast asleep. It is ten to seven. Miyuri sits by the tea table and opens a booklet she bought in a local bookshop. *Literati's Minomachi*. She soon closes it, and watches outside the window, resting her cheek on her hand. Beyond the window mirroring her transparent face, are an air conditioner, two empty plastic bottles of Coke, and an abandoned pot of green orchids. She is still thinking of the question. She knows what to ask, but she does not know whether to ask.

The man turns around on his futon, murmuring something, and then blinks his eyes. Just then the clock clicks seven o'clock. The timing gives Miyuri a smile.

"Slept well? I'm so hungry. Shall we go out and eat?"

between the imperial garden and temple street

I THOUGHT BETWEEN THE IMPERIAL GARDEN AND Temple Street there was a triangle lot. The Imperial Garden stretches north and south in a long rectangle and Temple Street runs along the east side of the garden, almost parallel, slightly deviating eastward thus forming a long narrow triangle lot between them. But all of my friends say there is no such space in the east of the Imperial Garden, and Temple Street runs straight like the hand of a compass.

I thought between the Imperial Garden and Temple Street there were a nameless gravel road along the narrow creek and a sandy gray wall without a street lamp, dark and quiet even during the day. In the creek trickles trifling spring water from north to south. Beyond the high wall, thick oak trees shade the road. The nameless gravel road starts from the small east gate of the garden and leads to a shrine in that narrow triangle lot. Taxi drivers sleep on the gravel road. They park their cabs along the wall and take a nap in early afternoon under the shelter of oak and maple. The bustle of downtown and the universities are three minutes away on foot. But the road is quiet. The air is dark and wet.

But my friends say there is no such silent spot behind the Imperial Garden.

I remember one early evening I was strolling down the nameless gravel road alone. It was early fall but the air was already cold behind the Imperial Garden. My feet crunched the gravel. I was watching my feet until I noticed a white Civic parked alone. It wasn't a taxi. I kept walking straight ahead. The sky was getting lower.

The oak leaves were turning black. There was something moving inside the car.

Taxi drivers don't move in their cars. They sleep. Through the windshield I saw somebody's back moving. A man—probably a college student, maybe I saw his profile, or maybe just his nose or forehead—he was clumsily shifting and twisting his body. Maybe I just imagined it. In the front seat he was shoving and sliding his shoulders and pressing his face against something in the dark. I am sure I saw his profile. But he didn't see me. I walked closer. The sky was getting darker, but I could still see the awkward movement of his arms. When he slid his shoulders, pushing his head down, a white round thing glowed in the dark through the windshield. It was a woman's face, with her eyes blank open. She was not stiff as the boy who was now butting her in the neck. She was still and dull like a celluloid mannequin. She did not blink. But her pupils moved. While her eyes met mine for a second, the boy was pressing himself hard against her and wasn't moving, maybe at a loss for what to do next. Her eyes seemed as if they had wanted to share something with me. This I still don't know. Whether she had something. What that something was. Maybe a complaint about her lover's clumsiness, or maybe just her boredom. Soon I walked past the car and left the unnamed gravel road. Maybe she was a mannequin.

Everybody tells me it was just my dream. Maybe a hallucination. People say I was frustrated, needed a lover. Skilled or clumsy.

Other times, I remember, somebody in the shrine would rake up the fallen leaves and burn them on the gravel road. She would put sweet potatoes and chestnuts on the gravel beneath the inflamed leaves. The chestnuts burst —the sound echoed in the Imperial Garden, sudden gun shootings afar. After that, a black circle would remain on the gravel. I used to stamp on it. Sometimes it was warm and sometimes it was wet and ashes stuck to my shoes.

But nobody else has seen it or stamped on the black circle of ash on the gravel. Except me. Or so they say.

The shrine was a small shrine that deified Sanjo Sanetomi, a duke who died in the last century, if my memory is correct. The shrine was called Pear Tree Shrine, but there was no pear tree on the site. The site was filled with bush clovers. There were some Japanese maple trees, too. People say the maple tree is most beautiful in November when it changes its color. But I know the maple tree is most beautiful in early June, just before the rainy season starts, while the leaves are still tender and young. When the color is not quite green. When half transparent under the sun. I used to walk in the shrine garden early in the morning. Probably at five o'clock. The elderly in the neighborhood were raking and watering the garden. They would chat around the dead grass gathered in a heap. My friends say there is no way I could see such a sight because I never wake up at five in the morning. That is true.

But I think I remember I saw it.

I thought there was a small well in the corner of the shrine. The well was in an arbor half hidden in the bush clovers. An electric pump drew water. The water was utterly odorless and tasteless. It was cold in summer and mild in winter. It was the only remaining spring well, which had provided water for the Imperial Palace in the old days. I remember I used to fill plastic soda bottles with the water and bring them home. I remember it took me twenty minutes from my apartment to the shrine and I still feel the weight and the coolness of the bottles against my forearms as I brought them back home, holding them like twin infants. I would make jasmine tea with the spring water. It smells sweeter and tastes milder with the spring water. My friends laugh at my story and say it must have been tap water. Your jasmine tea stinks. It's your daydream. They say Temple Street runs straight and there is no triangle space between the Imperial Garden and Temple Street, so there is no such well. I say there is. They say there isn't. I say is, and they say you go see, you go and check with your own eyes.

I thought there was a lean triangle spot between the Imperial Garden and Temple Street in Kyoto, but I have never returned to see that place. One morning I realized I was a murderer. I had slaughtered some person I had known and buried the corpse in a bamboo bush in my hometown, far, far away from Kyoto. The person had learned that I dreamt this dream so I had to kill him. The earth was soft as I dug with my bare hands. The spot I had buried the corpse had been round and darker than the rest of the ground. I suddenly remembered this one day in Kyoto. I knew the memory struck me suddenly in Kyoto because somebody had found the body in my hometown. Somebody must have found that person under the ground. Now dead. I was afraid they would come get me. I had to recall whether I had closed his eyes, whether I had put shoes on his feet, whether I had combed his hair. I couldn't remember. It was an awful feeling. You might have boarded a plane and you couldn't remember whether or not you turned off the gas before leaving home. I was frantic trying to recall whether I put shoes on him or not. I had to remember before they came to get me. I had tried to recall for a fortnight until another possibility came into my mind. A dream. Everything had been a dream from the beginning: I had strangled him, I had shaken him, bumped him against the windowsill, shaken him again violently, bumped him against the floor, then put my fingers into his throat, pulling his hair back and dragged him to the door. Then I had wrapped myself up in a woolen blanket and slept soundly. My feet had been cold.

The well in the shrine attracted many natives. It was a secret spot in the beginning but gradually word spread and people came to pump the tasteless, odorless water. On Sundays, there was a long line in front of the well. There was an apprentice cook from a three-star restaurant. He wore a white cotton suit and brought back a tankful of water. The water level was ebbing. The shrine put out a sign to regulate the amount of the water to less than three liters per person. Then people began to come with their families. The shrine put out a donation box. But it didn't help either.

I certainly have a good imagination, they say, I made up the whole story about one little well in an imaginary triangle spot between the Imperial Garden and Temple Street, which bends slightly eastward only in my imagination. I had to leave Kyoto awhile and I don't know what happened to the well. All I know is when I returned to Kyoto in April, when I came back to the dark unnamed gravel road, to the narrow triangle space with bush clovers, oak trees and maples, the well was still there in the arbor, but there was no one. The well was flooded with the immortal spring water. Tasteless and odorless. The shrine garden deserted. The place clean.

There was a black ash circle on the graveled road and it was cold and dry when I stepped on it. The fire must have been out for a long while.

People say go see. Go and see because there is no such place. I know there is a long triangle space between the Imperial Garden and Temple Street that slightly deviates to the east. Where taxi drivers sleep. They say go and see but I will never go back because if I do the dream will come true and they will come get me. I will never go and see.

dreamcave

IT LIVES IN THE HUMAN VESTIBULE, *AURIS INTERNA*, which is actually called the labyrinth, a bat cave, not a conchiferous ocean like some are led to believe. There it hangs upside down in your inner ear, the only dreaming organ of the human body. You dream every night. Every night you are in different bedrooms though you may not know it. You live in this bed & breakfast without knowing. The bed & breakfast so enormous with innumerable rooms, or rather, the number of rooms matches the number of your dream variations, which is forever unknown to the dreamer yourself since there are rooms you visit without ever knowing. For example, your dream of buying an exact number of seedless clementines at the market. You dream it almost every night, but the dream will not stick. Only seedless clementines accumulate under your bed. Your palms grow orange and you don't know why. Of course, the dream lasts for a flash of a second, one hundredth of a second at most. But for the duration of that particular dream sequence, you are in the seedless clementine room.

Thus your noctuary goes on: seedless clementines, sober handkerchief, skywalking, disjointed nudity, paraphrasable marsupial, sinistrous hand cream, varicosed vapor, promenading furbelows, the future of thalassocracy.... All the while the creature is wide awake in your vestibule, *chauve-souris*, the bald mouse, holding a vigil. It lives on the honeydew secreted from your *utricle* drop by drop, excreting wax, whose accumulation forms various shapes of stalactite. The pipistrelle inhabits there happy and comfortable, night after night, while you, the nocturnal bird of passage, the itinerant dreamer, roam from one bedroom to another, following the ultrasonic lead from the cave. Sometimes it gets too hectic for you to sleepwalk from one room to another, so you simply collapse and fall asleep in one room for the remains of the night.

And there are rare moments when the bat becomes fully awake all of a sudden, batting its fine, half-translucent patagia, yet at the same time confused about its own state of being, flounces about the cave, while you the dreamer almost emerge from the heavy water of nightmare, savoring the horror, slowly delineating the undulating border between the two worlds, trying to have them both at the same time and failing, wanting to catch yourself lying sweaty naked in one of the bed & breakfast bedrooms but also hoping the state of swimming in the shallow water of stupor to drag on as long as possible till your breath runs out. As you surface, the tinnitus becomes unbearable, pressing the dry warm air out of the cave, the bat starts out of your ear like a bat out of hell and flutters in the black air, oscillating, perfectly avoiding the walls, furniture, and you the dreamer whose head is still, buried in the pillow. The creature disturbs the air, churning the thick of the night, disturbing the darkness, and it is this tiny whirlwind that the down on your cheeks senses, that brings you the realization that you are sleeping with a bat in the belfry, that you are sleeping in one of the innumerable bedrooms at this bed & breakfast, that you are dreaming, and that the noctule lives in your vestibule, the labyrinth within. At this exact moment of your epiphany, the bat slashes the blackout curtain surrounding the silver screen inside your skull. A sinister grin flashes through the slit. An ultrasonic scream shatters the night. Your heart skips a beat. You wake up and you are in your old apartment. You don't recall anything about the bed & breakfast, that googolplex complex. You remember the creature, though. *Die Fledermaus,* the flittermouse. The false vampire, people sometimes call it. You caress your cheek, brooding on the breath of air it stirred.

Your life goes on. You completely forget about it. That it lives in your vestibule, in the only dreaming organ of your body. Until one day, your otologist tells you your left ear is full of wax. Needs a fix. Labyrinthectomy, that is. Before you swallow its meaning, she sticks a funnel into your ear, puts a few drops of thick liquid that numbs half your head. The otologist puts you under sedation. The last thought that flashes through your mind: a melon—a ripe melon rolls around in the kaleidoscope you peek in. The melon multiplies.

You wake up half deaf. The otologist yells at you, *don't worry it'll come back*. She proudly presents a kidney-shaped silver tray half full of wax and labyrinth, *your* labyrinth that resembles an umbilical cord or chopped clam meat. A tiny bat the size of your pinky nail lies there completely scatheless, long dead, its wings folded tight to its still chest. Tiny claws. *Now you can sleep without ever being disturbed by dreams*, your otologist says.

they did not read the same books

THEY DID NOT READ THE SAME BOOKS. IT WAS NOT because he was Japanese and she Taiwanese. It was not because, like he contends in his own writings, every reading is a unique experience. They both read in English. They read in the morning, they read during the day, but they read especially at night, lying supine and parallel on the wide bed, they read together and separately.

Their house stands a few blocks away from the lake, whose sweet water smells like the ocean. The water even moves tugged by the moon. On windy spring nights, one can hear the water roaring, crashing in the distance. Their house is small, wedged between equally modest houses shoulder to shoulder, looking up the clocktower. The tradition dictated that the city would ring the bell only when a person of importance passed away. Once someone petitioned the city to toll the bell for every death since everyone's life is equally valuable. But how can you live in world where the grand clocktower is ringing all day and all night like a madman who speaks nothing but the Truth? Someone is dying at the moment, at *this* moment, at *every* moment. So the city council voted to silence their clocktower altogether. That way, every life would be valued equally *and* people could forget about the shadow that tailed them until they looked back one day and got caught.

That morning, she drove their car. He had to take a taxi. Now he stands in the parking lot. In the middle of the parking lot wide open to the freeway is a red Toyota Evangelist, neatly parked inside the white rectangle drawn on the asphalt. The car is alone, without company, unlike other vehicles in the same lot.

They did not read the same books, but in their youth, they had often shared the same books, lending and borrowing, presenting books as gifts and borrowing them back, and passing library books to one another, often ending up paying late fees for one another. That had been a part of their long courtship.

Before moving into the small house near the lake, they would meet at the cinema every week, often Thursday, catching the last screening of this or that movie before it left town. Going to the cinema together was like reading the same book. Emerging from the cinema's cave, drenched in luminous shadows, she liked to keep the silver secret to herself. Whenever she closed her eyes, the back of her eyeballs would re-project the film on the hemispheric screen inside her scull. On the other hand, he liked to talk about the film they had just seen. He wanted to test his interpretation against hers. Since she had no such thing, she was dumbfounded that sound and image could be connected with abstract language in one's mind. His words poured into her head like sawdust. She would have gladly plugged her seven apertures if that had let her keep the movie in her head as long as possible. She was not sure anymore if they had seen the same movies. That was around the time when they moved into the small house together.

Books crawled into their house from everywhere—from the front door, backdoor, and windows, especially from the bathroom window, also from the mailbox and chimney. Slowly but surely the invaders had taken possession of the house. To their amazement, they had never brought home the same book separately. They had similar tastes in books and somewhat different interests.

She would become immersed in the books she was reading so wholeheartedly that she talked about them all the time, insisting he should read the same things, and he did indeed, and sometimes he was delighted, other times mildly disappointed, until he began to feel that picking up someone's recommendations was like following her imaginary footprints, encountering many N.B.s and exclamation marks and checks and lines and coffee stains and unidentifiable body hairs scattered over the passages. He often erased others' pencil markings left on the pages of library books, grunting and lamenting the decline of civility though sometimes he penciled in library books himself. He then would erase them all over himself, grunting and lamenting the burdens civil society imposed upon him.

She always felt the book in her hands at the moment was the most sensational thing, because as she lay there supine next to him, the book would do all sorts of things to her, something utterly unimaginable to the man lying next to her. She had reached the conclusion that the only way to sustain this secret pleasure and share it with him at the same time was to keep reading different books from him.

They did not read the same books, but sometimes, they read aloud to each other. There was not any set turn. Sometimes one would read for three nights straight, and other times neither of them would volunteer so they would return to their different books silently. They kept a few volumes of fairy tales, poetry and very short stories in the hollow between their pillows. At nights—mostly weekdays when they'd rather spare lovemaking—one would read a piece to the other. The other would grow impatient to read another him/herself. Or he/she would fall asleep before *they lived happily ever after*. It was a way to caress each other, a way to hold their hands as they walked through separate passages lying parallel, supine.

The city's clocktower illuminates the passage to the factory gate where nightshift workers silently gather. The clocktower keeps its silence. The sweet water ebbs and flows on the lakeshore.

They did not read the same books any more, but they knew exactly which book the other was reading. Or rather, because they knew exactly which book the other was reading, they never read the same books. One time, they both wanted to read Sir Walter Scott's novels one after another, like girls at a boarding school started to crave for strawberries all at once. He started with *Abbot* and went through the titles in alphabetical sequence, while she set about reading *Woodstock* and went up in reverse alphabetical order. After six months, they finally met in the middle, at *Ivanhoe*, which neither of them dared to read.

Ivanhoe still sits in the hollow between the two pillows. He lies supine on the wide bed alone, not reading. That morning, she drove their car to the clinic. She had had a new kind of headache. Soon they called him and he had to take a taxi. He drove their Evangelist back home. On his way, he thought of all the books he would have to read all by himself for years and years to come. Driving home, he was counting the titles. He was at sea. The freeway stretched forever. The cool white cotton sheet billowed out to the horizon. Once home, he had to start reading. Otherwise, he would never finish.

clarity

As if he had been living in someone else's dream…. That was how Lui felt at the end of summer in his sophomore year, in his boarding room in Kyoto when Aki asked him why he was into haiku.

Lui gave a coy smile. "I don't know, perhaps because things are too complicated for me to figure out. With haiku, you don't have to try to capture the whole world."

"Aha, so the world is a bunch of secrets for a smart ass like you," Aki sneered and reached for his coffee. "No, don't, don't… No, how many times do I have to tell you I don't want any sugar in my coffee?"

"Sugar is fuel for the brain." Lui laughed generously and handed a mug to his friend anyway, ignoring the girl sitting at Aki's feet. "You know, sometimes I'm afraid I may not be able to figure out anything in life," Lui said. He turned his face to the sliding doors facing south. The sunlight found its way deeper into the room than a month ago, when they had swum every day at the college pool. The sky over the wooden fence was powder blue. The clouds looked like thin streams of skim milk.

The mercury was up to thirty-three degrees Celsius. It was an autumn sky, but the air was humid, thick, still summer. He recalled the sky he had gazed at, floating in the pool—the true blue with heavy puff whites.

"Ugh, this coffee gives me a headache." Aki stuck out his tongue. His lean long face was well tanned after a month's swimming while Lui's skin remained pale. Aki handed his coffee to the girl, who took it without a word and sipped it, holding the mug in both hands.

This girl, Lui thought, is also a mystery—Why is she here with Aki? Why doesn't she ever speak? Why does Aki never acknowledge her?

"It's still too hot for coffee," Aki complained and licked the inside of his sugar-sticky mouth. "I'm sweating. Turn on the fan, man."

Lui obeyed him.

"Coffee is good all year around," Lui said. "Caffeine, nicotine, alcohol: the three major nutrients for college students." He himself did not smoke, however.

"Let's go get some beer then."

"It's a matter of blood circulation. I enjoy hot drinks any time of the year. I'm cold blooded. My hands are always cold," Lui explained.

Aki bent over and covered Lui's hand on his knee. It was cold indeed.

"You are inhuman. You must be a spy cyborg from North Korea. Lui, touch her hand. Even a woman has warmer blood than you." Lui did not want to, but he took her right hand, which she offered him without a word. She had finished Aki's coffee.

It's wet, he was startled, *it sticks*. But his hand did not get wet.

Lui had known Aki only for two months. Aki appeared in Lui's world a week before the final exams, to copy his notes from the Number Theory class. Lui had not remembered Aki from the class. Lui passed the course with a B minus and Aki with an A. Since then Aki started to hang around with Lui. Lui also began to pick up what people said about Aki.

Most of the gossip was about the girls he was with. There was a basic line, which everyone agreed on: he is always with a different girl. And there followed other rumors: he never dates girls in his college; he sells drugs to girls; an immense inheritance came to him on his father's death; he is a gigolo; he is gay; he is thirty-six; he is eighteen.... All Lui could say was that Aki was surely with a new woman every time Lui saw him. He rarely attended classes, never seemed busy. He was usually rambling about the campus with a girl. Lui often saw him sitting on the bench smoking a cigarette in front of the Arts building. A girl always sat next to him. He did not show up at any parties. He did not seem to have any friends. Or any family for that matter. He did not seem to have a job.

Lui tutored prep school students in Math and Physics twice a week. During the summer vacation, however, he had to teach every day and could not leave Kyoto, while most of his friends had gone home or abroad. Aki was around him for the whole summer. Aki followed Lui to the college pool every day in August. He would visit Lui's room and spend hours doing practically nothing. Lui lodged in an apartment in Nanzen-ji, behind the temple's grounds. His room was six tatami mats large, with a simple kitchen, a half bath, and no air conditioner. Books and magazines covered the floor. Aki would complain about the mess and the heat but still frequented Lui's place. A girl was always with him.

Finally, Aki would come wearing only shorts, baring his tanned boney shoulders, holding a paper fan in his hand. Lui refrained from nudity in front of his friend's girlfriends. He would go out to the public bath after they left his room.

Thus they summered together in Kyoto. By the time school resumed in September, they may have appeared to be close friends to others, though Lui knew hardly anything about Aki.

Lui's friends told him that Aki was taking advantage of him. Lui had to agree with them. It was always Aki who decided things and Lui just accepted those decisions. Lui had an alley cat that used to come up to his porch for fish bones or milk. It would no longer visit him because of the smell of Aki's cigarettes. Now Aki was his cat. He stayed in Lui's room whenever he wanted, stretched himseld rolling over on the tatami floor, scratched the sand walls, dictated to him, demanded drinks, and left him at night. Lui trusted in goodwill of humanity, and people liked him for that reason, but more often than not, he did not know what to do with individual human beings. While he had friends, he had been alone. Then along came Aki with his thin presumptuous smile, doing whatever he wanted to do with Lui. For the first time, Lui learned that he could deal with someone by being totally passive. This discovery paradoxically encouraged him to mingle with other human beings.

Once when Lui came home late from tutoring, he found a light in the temple yard—a small red glow that slowly flickered like a buoy pitching on the calm night sea.

It was Aki, who was looking up at the lofty, wooden gate.

"Hey, you're smoking by a National Treasure!" Lui yelled at Aki.

"Oh, am I?"

"Yes. Put it out! Or I will call the police," Lui said feeling giddy. "What are you up to, Aki?"

"It's so cool out here."

Just then a figure materialized out of the darkness and caught Lui's breath. A girl in a black suit was standing behind Aki.

"You're back from work? You look relaxed," Aki said to Lui, and drew out another cigarette.

"It is refreshing. All my petty worries are gone when I deal with those highschoolers. They are full of energy—mostly used in stupid ways, you know."

"You like'm, huh?"

"Yes, I love them, ah, but they are so...." Lui hesitated.

"So?" Aki giggled pushing his fist against his mouth. His cigarette—it was always a Hi-lite—stuck out between his fingers.

"So stupid!" Lui spoke out, then breathed deeply, and smiled. "It's like, preaching to a flock of chicks. Aki, do you want to have a drink at my place or go out?"

"No." He waved and bent over to put his cigarette out against the footstone of the National Treasure gate, at which Lui gave him a reproachful look. "We'll walk back home. I didn't know Nanzen-ji Temple was such a great place for a night walk."

"Yes. It's far more splendid at night, isn't it?"

Aki did not listen to Lui's last words. They walked away into the dark. Lui picked up the stubs on the ground and went home.

"I just can't trust that Aki guy." Nana was probably the twelfth person to warn him about Aki. "He's already spoilt himself and now it's your turn. You quit him or he'll screw you bad." She was his high-school friend in Kanazawa, graduated a year ahead. Lui blushed at her words but she did not notice. They were eating lunch at Cafe Mizuho. Fried rice with leek and bacon for Lui and spaghetti with baby anchovies and seaweed for Nana.

"Well..." Lui looked hard at the ceiling for a good minute then turned to her only to give an awkward smile.

Nana sighed. "What's wrong with you? You were the sharpest kid around, never hesitated. You were a brilliant student, a star long-distance runner. We all thought you had everything—of course you were a tyrant before, didn't care much about others, and we all envied you for that—how clear the world must have appeared to you. Now you're stupidly choosing words and lingering over everything. What's your problem?"

"I can't explain. Maybe that's the problem?"

Nana sighed at his remark. Lui admired Nana for her self-confidence and strong words. He could not speak so decisively any more. He had been having trouble making a clear statement of any sort.

Lui had been brought up in a small world where academic achievement was everything. In Kyoto, Lui first felt he had been thrown into a sea. Innumerable intelligent people, eccentrics, and far more ordinary people who thought they were unique, floating around him like tiny particles of debris. They paid little attention to each other. He discovered that he had hardly learned anything in his life. The university had seemed a vast opening to the ocean of knowledge, yet it was an isolated island. In the wooden boarding house that felt like it was outside time, he would sit at the window gazing at the skyline of the Higashiyama Mountains. He felt as if he had been observing the twilight world from the bottom of an old pond or a winter pool. It was about that time he started to publish his haiku in a small magazine. Seventeen syllables were barely enough for him to sort out his ineffable confusion.

Now Nana was talking about her plan for the November Festival at the university, the weeklong party on campus with thousands of visitors. Lui finished his last mouthful of fried rice and went to the counter to ask for a cup of coffee. He came back to their seats at the table by the glass wall facing the street. He heard something bump on the glass and turned to find Aki outside. A girl was beside him. Nana gave Lui a sidelong glance as if to test his attitude. Lui smiled at her, moved his lips in apology, and Nana looked at the cup he hadn't finished.

"There you are!" Aki laughed at Lui in a fluster. He was in faded skinny jeans and an unbuttoned banana-yellow Hawaiian shirt, showing his thin chest and narrow shoulders. Lui looked at Aki's sockless feet in rubber thongs. The girl standing by him wore a stiff-collared woolen dress and leather pumps.

"Do you want to play mahjong with us?" Aki said.

"No, sorry, I don't know how." Lui never tried to learn the Chinese table game. He was a good go player and an okay Chinese chess player.

"Who are the other players? Where are they?"

Lui at least knew the game required four players.

"My women. They are waiting for us at the mahjong parlor. You can come and watch us."

When Aki ordered Lui, Lui could not do otherwise. He walked back inside to pay his bill. Nana raised her eyebrows, but didn't say anything. The two men and the woman walked to the mahjong parlor. Lui kept twisting his bang around his fingers. He felt bad about Aki calling girls *my women*.

Aki suddenly addressed Lui, "What's wrong with you?"

Lui remained silent.

"You have something to say, Lui."

"You shouldn't call them 'my women,'" Lui said.

"What?"

Lui said it again: "They are not yours."

Aki sniffed, opened a new pack of cigarettes, and lit one up. "There's nothing wrong about calling my women *my women*." The girl gave Aki an absent look. The glance seemed to approve of his words. Lui felt worse. Lui had some idealistic notions about the relationship between a man and a woman, which Aki would laugh at. *Mutual respect. Independence and personal boundaries....* Mica, his first girlfriend at college, had left Lui because she thought to be loved by someone meant being bound by that someone. And according to her, Lui miserably failed to prove his love to her. After that bitter experience, he still could not give up his ideals.

Now Aki was giggling in front of Lui. "Have you heard of procreative disorder, Lui?"

"No. What's that?"

Aki almost choked on his laughter.

"Well, I read it in a journal...." And he started laughing again.

"What's so funny?"

"Somewhere in Europe—I forgot where—a certain chemical from birth control pills remained in female urine and polluted the water system, which turned the men in the area sterile."

Lui patiently waited for more to come, but Aki pulled a Hi-lite out of his pocket. He was having trouble lighting it because of his giggling.

"And so?" Lui waited for more to come.

"That's it. They named the pollution 'procreative disorder.' Isn't it wonderful?"

"Not really."

Aki gave up lighting the cigarette and crushed it in his hand. "Dammit! Don't you get it? Pollution used to imply destruction. Death. Now it can mean sterility, collective impotence. No more birth on earth. Clean murder. Man may go extinct being seedless. Isn't that a fascinating vision of doomsday?"

Lui shook his head. At least he learned that procreative disorder was the reason Aki was giggling all the while.

"I hate my genes," said Aki still amused.

Lui felt sorry for his friend. To dislike one's genes meant not only detesting oneself but also condemning one's parents and one's yet unborn children, but Lui did not take his words too seriously, so he remained silent.

There were six girls waiting in the mahjong parlor. Four of them had already started the first round on one table. Lui had never seen so many of 'Aki's women' together. Yet all of them seemed new to him. Aki and the other three sat at another table and started to shuffle tiles. Aki and Lui opened cans of Sapporo Draft.

"Are you coming to the party next Saturday?" Lui tried to change the topic.

"You know I won't." Aki turned up his eyes, with a new cigarette dangling at the corner of his mouth.

Lui knew he would not come. It was a blind date party with a group of students from a women's college in Kyoto. Lui was often counted in for those parties. His abundant dark brown hair to his chin, his clean face with large dreamy eyes, his sensitive looking fingers would draw girls' attention first, but once the conversation started, they would soon leave him for more entertaining boys. Still Lui went to blind date parties because he was needed in order to even out the numbers, and because he enjoyed being among unfamiliar, indifferent people.

"How could you go to such parties while picking faults in my words about my women?" Aki complained.

After watching two games, Lui walked home alone. He did not go to the bath that night. He felt too drunk to sit in the hot tub.

On Saturday at the party, Lui regretted coming when he found a girl he knew, one he had tutored in Math the year before. She recognized him at once and sat next to him during the whole party. He remembered her well, too. She was the worst student he had had that year. It was a miracle that she could get into any college. She had to review her Japanese reading skills before solving a factorization problem. But he liked her for one thing: she did not hesitate to ask questions.

She looked far different now as he had only seen her in her school uniform and without makeup before. She was liberated from Math, from school rules and from the pressures her parents and teachers put on her. When the party left the pub to move to a karaoke bar, Lui asked her for tea instead since he did not care for karaoke.

Having her first scoop of strawberry ice cream at a cafe on the Kamo River, she nearly made him spit out his coffee by saying, "I read your haiku."

He looked her in the eye. She was not joking.

"Where did you find the magazine?" Talking about his haiku always embarrassed him.

She shrugged. Feeling his ears hot, he blushed even more. She gave him a naughty grin and continued, "I like them. I especially like the last one: *Blue sky, White cloud—Everything is so clear.*"

This was the beginning of Lui and Mari's relationship. Things suddenly started moving around Lui. It was almost a month after the party before he saw Aki again. Summer was completely over.

"So have you scored with that woman?" This was Aki's malicious first response.

"No. But in any case that's none of your business," Lui honestly answered and went back to the integral problem he was preparing for the Math class. They were in his room again. Lui sat at the desk and Aki and a girl sat on a couple of flat cushions on the floor. The girl was very tall and appeared chilly in her short sleeves.

"You going out with that woman for a month getting any? What are you seeing her for?"

"For companionship, for instance?" Lui tried to sound generic.

"Yes?" Aki pursued.

Lui said no more.

"Well, we meet for companionship, too, don't we?" Aki smiled at the tall girl, who nodded back humming her approval. Lui didn't know if *we* meant to be Aki and the girl, or the three of them.

Aki went on, "So what else?"

"Why are we talking about this?" Lui turned his eyes away from the notebook to the two of them on the floor.

"Why not?" Aki shrugged. "People talk about my women behind my back. Now let's talk about your woman." He smiled his snaky smile. His thin red lips stretched. "We are all using them, I mean, women. Right?"

Lui opened his mouth to refute his judgment, but the words stuck in his throat.

"Yes, I see what you're thinking," Aki inturrupted in a louder, jollier voice, which then turned to a whisper: "I'm worse than you. You're innocent. You don't want to bind a woman. I'm the one who's using women, isn't that it?" As his smile grew, his hand touched the girl's long hair, and he brought a strand of it to his lips. His eyes were set on Lui, who averted his eyes. Aki's lips brushed her peach-skin cheek then her lips, still looking at Lui askance. The girl was staring straight at Lui. He told Aki to stop, to which Aki only replied by narrowing his eyes. Lui sprang up and left the room.

When he came back half an hour later, they were gone.

That fall, the Emperor was dying. He had been critically ill since September. Long lines of people waited overnight to sign their names in the official registry of sympathy in front of the Palace in Tokyo and the prefectural governments around the nation. People enjoyed playing a role in history by standing in the lines. The whole nation was merrily preparing for the upcoming days of mourning. Everyday, TV news reported how many milliliters of blood His Majesty was discharging from his bowels and how much had been replaced by transfusion, which reminded Lui of a weather report. By the time every drop of this man's blood was exchanged for other people's blood, and that blood was exchanged for more blood, Lui had arrived at the idea that the Emperor was not a person, but a vacuum. No, what was called the Emperor was not the vacuum, but all the events and people whirling around the vacuum. He was an improbable being that existed only when its surroundings became active.

What remains after he passes away? Only memory remains. History does not tell us who he was. Lui remembered his father's words on their way to Grandfather's funeral: a man's soul vanishes from the earth not when he dies but when his children die. A soul is not infinite, but it remains as memory in a few people's hearts for a short period. In whose memory would the Emperor remain? *Not mine*, Lui thought, gazing at the TV monitor absentmindedly. And what secrets would He carry into His vast, lonely tomb?

The November Festival had come with the first frost. Japanese maples had changed their colors overnight. Their leaves as small as a newborn's hands shaded stone-paved approaches to shrines and temples on the hill of Mt. Yoshida.

Lui had been dreaming frequently. He stayed in bed after he woke up in expectation of some vision. Usually he fell asleep again after a while and dreamt a couple of more loosely connected threads of images, often nightmarish. Those dreams in the late morning developed most vividly. Finally he would wake up slowly recollecting the fragments of dreams. This lazy habit put him in bed twelve hours a day. He could not get what he wanted from these dreams. They were supposed to provide him with insight. But they all vaporized in the daylight. Lui believed dreams were another hemisphere of human life—if you did not explore your dream life, you were only half alive. But the current result was only too much sleep, which made him only more melancholic.

Lui and Aki escaped the crowd. It was the third day. Lui had just seen Mari off at the bus stop. He had guided her around the campus all day. After Lui and Aki passed the red gate of Yoshida Shrine at the back of the university, they entered another world. The narrow path was deserted. The air was crisp and cold and the sky was clear.

"I wish I was faster," Lui said ascending the gentle stone steps to Yoshida Shrine, following Aki.

"Why? You are a fast runner. You swim well. Isn't that enough?" was Aki's loud remark. He kept going ahead of Lui in wide gait. He was not with a woman that day.

"I mean I want to be quick enough to seize the images in my dreams before they flee from me."

"I never dream," Aki confessed in a pleasant voice.

"No kidding."

"I don't. I never do. I'm dead asleep every night," Aki said.

"You can't be. That's impossible."

Lui stopped walking. His eyes grew large and gloomy. The prospect of dreamless nights sounded wonderful yet full of despair. Aki stopped and turned around to face Lui, pushing his hands in the pockets of his long unbuttoned coat against his body to screen the wind. He was smiling. His narrow eyes became narrower. Aki was looking at Lui, who was staring at damp crimson leaves on the moss between stones. *Nights without dreams*, Lui thought, *if such things could happen.*

"Yes, such things happen. It's true." Aki's voice turned soft, and dark. Damp. He put his arm around Lui's shoulder, a surprisingly friendly gesture for this man. "Come," he said, "Come with me." And he was off.

When Lui turned up his face, Aki was striding up the dirt slope by the stone steps. The rhythmical sound of his steps on dry twigs and fallen leaves was fading away.

"Come follow me, Lui!" Aki yelled keeping up his pace. He did not turn back.

Lui watched Aki's gray coat flapping as he went up. When Aki disappeared among tree trunks at the top of the steps, Lui skipped steps running after him, calling his friend's name.

They went up through a series of vermillion shrine gates, through golden ginkgos, narrow slopes, and stone-paved paths, then came to the east side of the hill, shady in the late afternoon. Among the shrubs and maple trees, beyond mossy stone walls, stood aged houses, mingled with old-fashioned boarding houses.

Aki led his bewildered friend into a desolate house. Its dreary garden told Lui that once there had been residents who had cared for its winding pine, an aged pomegranate over the fence, an *Osmanthus fragrans* spreading its branches above the bathroom window at the peak of its scent, its golden blossoms scattered over the leaves fallen on the dry moss. An out-of-shape granite lantern and a nandina grown wild stood by a shallow dry pond, full of leaves and dying weeds, edged with rough stones.

Aki was waiting for Lui at the open door.

Inside the Victorian style house, he could hardly find a trace of human life. He smelled dust, but the house was clean. The foyer was spacious and unfurnished.

Most of the rooms were vacant. In the dining room, he saw a table and a pair of chairs on the hardwood floor. A coffee-stained bowl and a spoon were left on the table.

There was a lacquered folding screen in the next room. The space behind the screen must have been where Aki slept. A futon was left spread on the cold floor. Trash was scattered around. A couple of ragged towels hung over the screen. His space was miserably small in this vast place.

"Welcome to my house!" Aki rubbed his hands.

Lui gathered the collars of his jacket. It was colder inside. Aki lit his last Hi-lite and threw away the crushed package. It bounced off the screen, but he did not look at it.

"It took me a while to get rid of things after my father died," he said, walking around in the empty living room. Ashes snowed onto the hardwood floor from his Hi-lite. He was staring at his, and Lui could see Aki was choosing his words.

"I'll move out of this goddamn place soon, but I've got to show it to you before I leave." The cigarette fell from his fingers. Aki stabbed it out on the hardwood floor and pulled his head back. "Let's go upstairs."

The rooms upstairs were carpeted and bath towels were spread on the floor. Aki stamped on them carelessly. There was a large aluminum tub on the tiled floor of the bathroom. Next to the bathroom were a pair of French doors to a linen closet.

After glancing at Lui a second, Aki jerked the doors open.

Lui found a closetful of colorful plastic sheets piled up. They were flat, and cut into the same size, carefully folded and stacked in four rows in upper and lower piles.

Colors varied; the sheets were painted, black and beige being the dominant colors. Looking at them closely, Lui found that the texture was neither plastic nor vinyl; it had a more rugged surface and was made of several materials. Smooth part, fine yarns, hard tips, drapery things.... It was difficult to recognize a pattern or design in the piles of material, but Lui could recognize some faces printed on the sheets. Eyes and noses.

"These are my women," Aki said with a gleeful smile.

Things began to dawn on Lui—he told himself to leave this place immediately, but was frozen. The backs of his eyeballs throbbed.

Carefully pulling out a sheet from the top of the pile, Aki unfolded it and held it up. Some wrinkles had distorted its shape, but it was a life-size female figure, flat and dry as wallpaper.

"Let's see which one is your type." Aki dropped the thing on the floor, where it crumpled like worn pajamas. He browsed through the upper pile, murmuring, "I know your type—sensible, petite, no makeup, wears a skirt... Uh, this one's got mold all over! And her clothes! Totally obsolete. I'll dry her in the sun. There. Lui, how about this one? That's your type. I know that." He pulled a sheet out of the stock.

Lui felt like vomiting from the moment he saw the things. Now he felt even worse because the thing, the woman, Aki was holding, was definitely his type. The type of woman he would prefer to be with if he had had to choose, except that her body was flat and wavy like a damp veneer.

Humming the tune from a TV cooking show, an unlit Hi-lite from a fresh pack dangling from his lips, Aki brought an empty kettle from the kitchen downstairs and filled it with hot water in the bathroom.

"Now..." He carefully folded the thing to fit in the aluminum tub and poured the hot water.

The vapor swooshing out of the tub was so thick that it filled the cold bathroom in an instant, and Lui could hardly see anything. Out of the immense steam emerged the woman, unfolding herself into three dimensions. No sound, no odor. Only the heat of vapor filled the room. *The Birth of Venus*. She was dressed in a cream silk blouse and a black polka-dot skirt. Her skin was creamy and glowing. Soft wavy hair framed her small face. Dark cherry wet lips. Pink fingertips. She was steamy fresh, clean and beautiful. She stepped out of the tub by herself, and looking straight at Aki, called her man's name. Then, a thud.

Lui had fainted.

A month passed. It was a quiet Christmas week. The Emperor had been dying a slow death. Lui had been trapped in a nightmare. Getting out of bed required greater effort every day. He would stay in bed fifteen hours a day. Fragments of various dreams mingled and confused him, the waking world was becoming less and less meaningful to him.

Lui had been feeling guilty. But of what? He could never tell. He kept telling himself, *I'm the one who holds his secret. I could tell the rest of the world what I've seen.* Only if he could tell! In reality, he was the one tormented by guilt and Aki was more cheerful than ever. He was still rambling around with his dry, steamy women. Lui felt like he was the one whose secret had been threatened.

"Are you okay?" Mari asked Lui for the third time as they walked up a path along the creek in Higashiyama.

"I'm fine." Then he lost his words. His eyes grew bigger and his pace paler. She reached out her white mittened hand to his cheek. The mohair mitten reminded him of cloud, then steam. It hurt him. Mari felt his head sink gradually onto her furry palm. A wind blew his hair across his face covering it. An aching pleasure filled her as she held his head's weight. Lui closed his eyes.

In a small windowless cell, a sausage machine was hard at work. It was steam-engined and soundless. Shrunken salted lamb intestines shrunken in salt writhingly swelled yard after yard like a Gorgon's hair. The machine produced a heap of flesh-filled intestines and now it was coiling up and up. Here and there were eyeballs, teeth and hair among the pink ground flesh in the tube. The sight was dim in the growing cloud of steam. The heat was unbearable.

Lui opened his eyes; Mari had combed away his hair over his face with the other hand and had kissed the edge of his lips. Lui wanted to hold her tight and weep, but his eyes were too dry.

"Your face is so cold," she whispered, "And your hands, too."

The campus was busy getting ready for the winter vacation. Lui was sitting at the top bench in a lecture hall with his friends after the class. They were planning their ski tour to Nagano.

When Nana found Lui, he was resting his chin on the desk like a well-fed monkey. She hit his back, and he let out a shriek, which frightened her. Lui twisted his trunk to face Nana.

"Wow, Nana, it's you. You scared me."

"*You* scared *me*. How's everything? You've lost your weight," said Nana.

"Desperately fine. I'm leading an incredibly fantastic life."

Nana frowned at his pleonasm. She sighed slightly and put her hand on his shoulder blade. "Well, will I see you at the Christmas reunion tonight? Are you bringing your girlfriend?"

There was a chattering noise echoing far up the hallway.

The noise became louder as it came closer to the lecture hall, accompanied by random footsteps. There were at least twenty or thirty people approaching.

"What's that? Radicals?"

"They must be demonstrating against Imperialist Christmas Commercialism," someone joked.

The two opposing groups of leftist radicals on campus had been active again over the past several months. One group had clubbed a member of the other group to death in spring, and one group had allegedly set fire to the gymnasium in early summer. Those in the room stood up alarmed but gradually went back to their seats as the noise turned out to be female voices.

The voices chanted: *where's Akira, where's Akira?*

Lui rose up and strode over the back of the bench, his hand on Nana's shoulder.

Through the two open doors of the lecture hall, they saw about a hundred young women clamoring, jostling in the hallway. Every woman was looking in every direction, asking each another: *where's Akira, where's Akira?*

Lui yelled to Nana, "Will you please call Mari and tell her I can't come. Tell her I'm terribly sorry!" and he disappeared.

He ran through the buildings, stairs, yards, calling his friend's name just like the hundred young women. When he came back to where he had started—the yard in front of the Arts building—he saw Aki relaxed at his regular bench. Lui stood in front of him, breathless.

"Hey, what's up?" Aki said. "I'm glad you came to see me again."

Wrinkles gathered around his eyes when he smiled.

"I didn't know your name was Akira."

"Akira means clarity, as you may know," Aki explained.

No, that was not what Lui intended to discuss. He tried again.

"What did you do to them?"

Aki shrugged. "Why, it's the holiday season. A good occasion to consume a bunch of them at once."

"They are marching on campus looking for you," Lui said.

"I know." Aki shook his head in feigned disappointment. "Maybe I went too far. I couldn't imagine how bulky a hundred women could be. They are so compact and thin when they are dry, you know, Lui."

He knew.

"You'll come to my house tonight, won't you? It's a bit boring, just me and a hundred women. You can bring your woman with you, too, if you want."

There was no way he would take Mari there.

The garden was dead except for a few evergreens and the house had not changed since Lui had visited a month ago. The two men and a hundred women, packed in the house, played games, drank, danced, sang and chattered. The clamor of the party was jovial, and so was the host. Lui felt that the noise was still and orchestrated. Aki took Lui to the bathroom, closed the door and shared a bottle of champagne just between the two of them, sitting on the edge of the bathtub. Lui sneezed sniffing up the bubbles of the drink. He'd got a chill from perspiration.

"God bless. Merry Christmas." Aki toasted and opened the door and yelled at the women outside to shut up.

They did not. It was after midnight. The body heat of the crowd kept the house warm. The two talked about school, their childhood, their hometowns, and other trivial things. Lui was surprised to learn that Aki had actually had a childhood, a rather ordinary one. Aki was more enthusiastic than ever. The night went on.

When the clock on the bathroom wall clicked six in the morning, Aki opened the door and nodded at Lui to follow. They pushed themselves through the flock into the living room. The women showed no fatigue. They were still playing and chattering. Lui felt a little drowsy.
Aki pulled aside the curtains of the porch windows facing east. They waited for dawn.

A ray beamed through the glass, lighting a path of dust in the room. When it landed on one woman, a blue flame leapt out of her chest, immediately covering her body. She was still talking. Soon the pale flare spread in the room, then all over the house. The air was filled with transparent sapphire. Aquamarine waved and swirled all around. The overwhelming icy blaze reflected the sunrise swallowing and freezing the two men. The women evaporated one by one, talking, dancing, and singing.

By the time the sun rose over the hill, they had all vanished.

Aki said, "Let's walk outside."

Outside, it was snowing and the sun was shining. The odd weather was a perfect ending for their strange party. The neighborhood was still asleep. Aki walked ahead, did not care about Lui as usual. Lui followed Aki, thinking, *I must be living in someone else's dream.*

"Blue cloud! White sky! Everything so clear!" Aki's breath steamed into the air.

"What are they?" Lui finally asked.

"They are my women," Aki said, giving his usual answer.

Then he paced down to walk beside Lui and said that he had first seen them when his father was dying, that his father had received them from *his* father, who had inherited them from *his* father and so on, that no one knew where they'd come from, nor when, nor *why*, that the patriarch was destined to live with the women, that they'd evaporate when the sun rose unless one first became a mother.

"That's all I know. But that's enough." Then Aki bent to look at Lui's face, saying, "Do you remember you solved a determinant problem in Kudo's Calculus class in June, right before the rainy season? You proved the determinant impossible using a *reductio-ad-absurdum*. Only in five lines— and it took me two pages, forty-six lines to prove the same problem! It was an impressive job. It was so simple, clear and beautiful. Do you remember that?"

Lui remembered that he had solved problems a few times on the blackboard, but not the one Aki was talking about. "I was lucky with that one."

Aki cast his rapt look afar and told Lui that it was the first time he had noticed Lui. That week his father had revealed the secret to him. The skeleton in the closet.

Aki added, "You said to me that there are so many mysteries you don't understand. You can't—you never can. But there they are. That is clear enough. There is nothing to wonder at. Nothing to dream about."

When Aki had seen the women in the closet for the first time, all the riddles, wonders, and delusions of the world must have vanished for all their absurdity. Everything was concrete. *The sky was white, the cloud blue, everything was so clear.* The women—they were his mothers, his sisters and his wives—they were all *his* women.

Burn every mother, every sister and every wife. A flare a day! To the last piece! Explore his pedigree from the very beginning to the dead end by reduction to absurdity. Aki was enthusiastically exhausting his fate. He did not need to *know* the women. What did he need to worry about while puffing up these women in the steam and seeing them blaze off in the dawn? Aki had cheerfully, even passionately, embraced his reality, this imposed vision of his world.

"Lui, I have a favor to ask."

Lui looked up at Aki, surprised at his unusually modest attitude. Aki was smiling as usual.

"Please see me through, will you? Watch everything I do and everything that comes to me. Okay, Lui?"

Lui nodded. Failing to look at Aki's face anymore, Lui just nodded and nodded again.

* * *

Two years later a local newspaper briefly reported the double suicide of a college student and a woman.

my earshell gondolier

There is a cage in downtown Providence in front of the City Hall. A dome-shaped aviary, or a circus lion cage. There is a Chinese boy inside, at least he appears to be Chinese, but he could be Burmese, for instance. There is a Chinese family that passes by every so often. This is a genuine Chinese family. They stop by the cage and say goodmorning to the boy. He is a famous child prodigy. The boy climbs on the cage to let the world know that he is. Then he comes down and wants to kiss the family. A kiss on everyone's lips. Father, Mother, Daughter, and Son. He has thick, arching eyebrows and a faint downy mustache. The family says goodbye.

The piano concert takes place in the Church early in the morning when the city is wrapped in the mist from the bay. Inside the narrow chapel, townspeople sit shoulder to shoulder, hip to hip, and listen to a hallucinatory fugue.

It is four-handed. Hands almost catch one another on the keyboard but never do. The white keys of the piano made of mother of pearl diffuse the light when knocked by four hands that belong to identical twin brothers. They are almost fifty years old but small, lean, and youthful, like dainty actors transplanted from a silent film. They are just too happy there is sound and it travels to other people's ears in this world. Before that, they could only hear one another.

The Chinese boy is released when there is a piano concert at the Church. The City Warden unlocks the cage and the boy bounces across the Plaza and marches down to the Church barefoot. He walks in in the middle of the performance. He walks down the aisle, yawning, like a child in pajamas still dragging his blanket. No one is bothered by the boy's entrance. The audience is too enthralled by the sprinting particles of light echoing on their squinting faces. The boy climbs onto the stage.

The four-handed fugue goes on.

There is a beautiful child, I say a child since I cannot distinguish its sex, sitting behind the identical twin brothers. It is a page-turner. But the twins always play from memory— nothing escapes their shared mind—so the beautiful one remains seated with its hands on its knees, its gaze straight. There is a rumor among the townspeople that there is an absolutely beautiful child sitting behind the four-handed twins, so beautiful it pierces your eyes, but the townspeople have never seen the child as their view is obstructed by the piano and the twin brothers, and the child never stands up to turn the pages. When the music is over, the child slips away.

When the Chinese boy walks up onto the stage, he passes by the piano and the twins and stands in front of this utterly beautiful child and thrusts his hip toward it. He just woke up and his cock needs something to rub against. A boy grows up in the cage in the City Plaza and townspeople passing by teach you every beastly way to make you a full-grown man, so what can you expect? That's the boy's education.

The beautiful child remains seated. The fugue goes on. The light twinkles. In fact, the way the boy presses himself, it is kind of a gentle nudge, in the sleepy morning way, and there is this dreaminess dripping from his body that smells good like a baby. The odor stays with him only for a fleeting moment when he wakes up. After a while, he stinks of dust, mucus, pimples, and semen like any other boy for the rest of the day. The beautiful one sits still. There is no way, nothing, to know how it is feeling, what it is thinking, so one could only guess. It does not seem to mind. It may not be a page-turner after all. Its sole job might be being rubbed against behind the four-handed twins by the Chinese prodigy kept in the lion cage.

The boy does not dwell on the beautiful thing. He walks to the other piano in the far back of the stage, a small pearl-grey piano, its wing already propped open, but first he has to fill his empty stomach, so he sits on a long bench in the corner of stage left, next to the piano. A cozy nook whose wall shields him from the audience. The moment he seats himself at the bench, the City Valet discreetly enters from stage right, holding a silver tray. The Valet leaves the tray on the Chinese boy's lap and withdraws. The boy feasts on the breakfast, ravished by the melting yolk of a half-boiled egg, pieces of fresh baguette and salted butter from Normandy, the cherry compote over fromage blanc redolent of the childhood garden he has never possessed, and let us not forget the white coffee, too strong for a child of his age, with one lump of sugar. He licks all his fingers carefully before palming the coffee cup.

This is almost like an infinity, the duration for the Chinese boy to finish the breakfast while the four-handed fugue by the silent film twins goes on and the townspeople in the Church think of this impossibly beautiful child behind the piano.

Then the fugue ends abruptly. Before the audience can applaud, the Chinese boy starts his music, which is, of course, a fantasia.

One by one and measure by measure, men and women in the Church go out like a light. They turn spineless and collapse over one another to the continuous chromatic ascendance, and the music reaches its climax in the locked chamber of their velvety phantasm while the sound of the abalone piano scintillates in the Church, the sound which may not exist, which may have vanished altogether in the morning mist of the collective swooning.

Time flies. Night comes in fastforward in the City of Providence as giant crows swoop down on pinnacles. From the damp blackout of the narrow chapel, townspeople emerge in twos and threes into the serene summer evening or the gritty winter night, in either case the salty wind blowing hard against whichever direction they are walking to. Outside, yellow gas lamps blotch the night, and the townspeople finally share a faint sense of brotherly emotion, something yet too unripe to be called love.

People scatter home down the illuminated streets and the Chinese family passes by the lion cage in front of the City Hall as they did the day before. There is a Burmese boy inside, at least he appears to be Burmese, but he could be a Thai, for instance. The boy climbs on the cage to let the world know that he is. He is a famous child prodigy. The Chinese family stops by to say goodnight to the boy. The Burmese boy comes down. He wants to touch the Chinese family. He thrusts his hands out. He gives a shallow embrace to each one of them, Father, Mother, Daughter, and Son. The Burmese boy has slim, long fingers. His lips are full and shaped like a gondola.

People of Providence! Indulge in your ephemeral sleep, for you sleep only in your dreams.